HOSPITAL CALL

Julie Alnaker was rich, young, and lovely. She and Toby Grant, who recently qualified at the Central, had been childhood sweethearts, grown up together. But now Julie was engaged to Rupert Ferris, an eligible architect of whom even Julie's mother approved. Julie was injured four days before her wedding in a riding accident and with Toby being on call was the first doctor to reach her and the first to realise that Julie might never walk again...

HOSPITAL CALL

Hospital Call

by

Elizabeth Harrison

Dales Large Print Books
Long Preston, North Yorkshire,
BD23 4ND, England.

British Library Cataloguing in Publication Data.

Harrision, Elizabeth
        Hospital call.

        A catalogue record of this book is
        available from the British Library

        ISBN   978-1-84262-732-7 pbk

First published in Great Britain by Hurst and Blackett Ltd.

Copyright © Elizabeth Harrison 1975

Cover illustration © Jake Gara by arrangement with
Arcangel Images

The moral right of the author has been asserted

Published in Large Print 2010 by arrangement with
Watson, Little Ltd.

Dales Large Print is an imprint of Library Magna Books Ltd.

Printed and bound in Great Britain by
T.J. (International) Ltd., Cornwall, PL28 8RW

CONTENTS

CHAPTER ONE

A Wedding at Alnaker Hall

On Saturday the picture gallery was opened in aid of the county branch of the Red Cross. Tickets cost a bomb, but the Alnaker pictures were renowned, and sherry on arrival, followed by a buffet lunch, were to be thrown in.

Max Alnaker himself put in one of his appearances, could be seen standing under the Annigoni portrait of Veronica, talking to Jo Grant – since the pictures were very valuable indeed – about the security side of the occasion. A small, squat man with an outsize personality, in the City Max was feared and respected. Down here, though, in his own countryside, they were inclined to take him for granted, their attention focused on his wife.

For Veronica Alnaker had been one of the first of the famous post-war models to take fashion by storm. In the early fifties her supercilious beauty had stared haughtily from all the magazines as well as from hoardings and posters everywhere. At that period models had been expected to be poised, elegant and, above all, scornful. Veronica's sculptured beauty was still, now she was in her middle forties, much photographed, she remained thin as a rake, and certainly knew to a nicety how to glare dispassionately down her lovely nose.

Her daughter Julie had inherited neither the looks nor the temperament. Quiet, intellectual, inclined to bouts of silence, she had pleased them at school, but continued to disappoint her mother. 'My funny little blue-stocking of a daughter,' Veronica would introduce her indulgently to her London friends, and only Julie knew how often the indulgence could wear thin.

Today was typical, Julie thought, with suppressed irritation. Far from wearing, as her mother had arranged, the charming ankle-length Tana lawn, ruffled, sprigged with blossom, perfectly suited to this lunch party in the gallery, there she stood, hair tied back casually, in yet another of her inevitable trouser suits. At least, though, she had turned up on time, evidently intended to carry out her assignment.

For Julie had been brought up with these

famous pictures, and although she knew that they were beyond price, virtually uninsurable, to her they were more like old family friends. And because she loved them, she always made – even Veronica admitted it – a superb guide to the gallery.

Today she was particularly brilliant. For Toby was there. His eyes met hers with startled admiration, with an awareness she was sure she could not be imagining. With him at her side, Julie surpassed herself as she led the visitors through the gallery. Among them was Rupert Ferris. He was riveted – and not by the pictures alone. He felt the stirrings of a quite separate excitement.

Suddenly the quiet Alnaker girl revealed a side of her personality he had never suspected. Her humorous, vivid, racy comments on the pictures and their subjects not only brought past centuries to life, but brought Julie herself alive for Rupert. While she showed him a line of Alnakers stretching back into history, he saw something for himself she knew nothing about. For Julie was every inch an Alnaker. He was struck by the regularity with which her features appeared in portrait after portrait, stretching unmistakably back through Victorian, Regency and Georgian days to Stuart and even Tudor

11

times. There she stood, in green corduroy, dark hair caught at the nape of her neck with a velvet bow, slim fingers – ringless, he saw with a surge of optimism – pointing out details in the pictures. And there in the portraits she could be duplicated. Rupert looked from Julie to the portraits, back to Julie again, and stretching across five hundred years he saw the same face, the same slight frame. A sensitive face, pale complexion, narrow curling lips, a small squashed nose with wide nostrils and a platform at the tip. A peasant's nose, you might have assumed, until you studied the Gainsboroughs, the Lely, the Van Dyck and the Nicholas Hilliard miniatures.

Rupert, of course, was enormously lucky to be there at all that Saturday. No one else in the firm had ever been invited to one of Veronica Alnaker's week-ends. 'You're made, my lad,' the senior partner told him, half scoffing, half enviously. For Rupert was an assistant in the firm of architects who had the Alnaker Hall contract, and while the occasion itself was an experience for him, the effect on his career might be phenomenal. For it seemed Veronica had taken to him. She had had him to dinner once or twice when the numbers needed making up, now at last had invited him to this week-end house party.

The week-end ran true to form. Veronica seldom did anything by halves. As usual, there were twenty or thirty guests staying overnight, and their visit had been co-ordinated with this charity function in the gallery. House guests had to make do with the same sherry and buffet lunch on Saturday as the paying visitors, and were expected, in addition, to help the staff push the food and drink round. A week-end at Alnaker Hall might be a privilege, but was seldom a rest cure. As long as you pulled your weight you would, so to speak, be fed and watered.

Hence Toby's presence. Veronica would not normally have tolerated him as a week-end guest – nor was he one, though he had been, at Max's insistence, invited for dinner. Afterwards he had to return to the local hospital, St Mark's in Halchester, where he could be on call at the accident unit from midnight.

And a good thing too, Veronica considered, watching him – tall, bony, gangling, his fair hair on the long side, and still with a student's untidiness, though they said he was qualified now. She was not in favour of Julie and Toby Grant seeing too much of one another. When they had been children it had been a different matter.

Of course, there had never been any lack of voices to point out that in adult life Lord Alnaker's daughter and Jo Grant's son must inhabit different worlds. The situation, too, was complicated by the fact that Veronica had never been able to stand Jo. For years he had been in charge of the transport at the Hall – he had been Max's transport sergeant in North Africa in 1943 – and recently Max had asked him to organize the new security system. Many of the staff alleged that during Max Alnaker's frequent absences it was Jo rather than Veronica who ran the estate. Even so, it would still take some sort of quiet revolution to fit Toby Grant to be the husband of the Hon. Julia Alnaker.

Nowadays, Toby himself had more doubts as to his eligibility than he had ever known when he was younger. If he had dreamt, all those years ago when he had left the Hall to study medicine at the Central London Hospital, that one day he would return in triumph to claim his childhood love, he had imagined her there, waiting for him, much as he had always seen her, about four feet high in gumboots, muddy jeans and sweater. Now that he was qualified, six months as Adam

14

Trowbridge's house surgeon at the Central behind him, he discovered, somewhat to his astonishment, that the passing years had left their mark on Julie too. Suddenly she had become not only beautiful but quite staggeringly sophisticated, so that he knew himself gauche, clumsy, incoherent, beside her, could no longer pretend not to understand what they all meant when they said she was not for him.

Of course, he'd changed too. He was sure of that. He was very different now from the boy who had left to make his name in London. Medicine had taken him, used him for five strenuous years, was continuing to demand all that he had to give. Even his first few weeks in the accident unit down here at St Mark's had shaken him. The practice of medicine had a habit of doing this to its recruits, of course, and it was far from the first time Toby had experienced the sensation. In the wards and clinics at the Central, in the theatres, he had often faced an ordeal that stretched him to his limits – and beyond. But always then he had known the entire resources of one of London's most famous teaching hospitals to be behind him, ready to be summoned instantly. Here, though – out on the motorway with the

15

ambulance, for instance – he had only himself to depend on. Life or death could be a matter of a moment or two, and a split second indecision could lose a life.

Under these conditions, the packed days had vanished with little chance to think about Julie, let alone see her. This Saturday had been his first day off in three weeks, and he had gone out to the Hall – only to discover, of course, that he had landed himself in the thick of one of Veronica's ghastly week-ends.

The day wore on in typical Alnaker Hall style. After the buffet lunch, and the dispersal of that intake of paying visitors to their cars, everyone adjourned to the gardens, open until six, also for Red Cross funds. Half Halchester was there, half the county too. Tea was served in the buttery, and all guests and staff were expected to remain on duty. (Circulate, circulate, Veronica had urged them.) She herself, radiant in a long garden-party gown of beige chiffon, a great Edwardian hat covered in somewhat unlikely beige roses shading her eyes, talked non-stop, made the rounds indefatigably – kept an eagle eye out for defaulters, too. Max Alnaker was one. He'd had more than enough of the week-end already, prowled impatiently for a while, at length slipped away to talk to Jo Grant in his office.

Julie went with Toby to help out with the teas in the buttery, a nice straightforward job, they both agreed, after the morning's demanding session in the gallery. Finally at nearly six o'clock they were able at last to sit down together at one of the gay little tables, have a cup of tea themselves.

Changing for dinner afterwards in her own private rooms in the Gatehouse, Julie was elated. For once, instead of climbing hurriedly into the easiest dress she had, she took her time, sprayed herself with perfume, arrayed herself in her most extravagant creation, one of Mark Midwinter's superb designs, its fluid lines and brilliant cutting underlining the grace that was an essential part of Julie's charm. That night there was to be a formal dinner in the great dining hall, crested silver gleaming, cut-glass sparkling, the candles lighted in the branching candelabra.

Afterwards they danced in the picture gallery, beneath the Annigoni and the Lely, the Van Dyck and the Gainsboroughs. Julie floated through the evening in a cloud of joy, dancing with Toby until nearly midnight. He had to leave then, as he was on call at the

17

accident unit for the next forty-eight hours. But the dancing continued, until two in the morning, and Julie found herself with Rupert, lost again in a haze of delight.

First Toby, holding all her affection from a shared childhood, and now Rupert. He was far better looking than Toby, of course, older too, dark and smooth where Toby was fair and undeniably rumpled. Rupert, new and exciting, sparked an instant response in her that surprised her by its power. Surely she couldn't be going to fall in love with this stranger?

On Sunday morning they rode in the park and the woods – Max and Julie, accompanied by half a dozen of the week-end guests, including Rupert, gingerly astride for, he told her honestly, the first time since pony-trekking holidays as a schoolboy. 'Years ago, I'm afraid. I'll probably disgrace you by falling off.'

'Do come,' she said.

It was enough.

In the summer woods the sun filtered at odd angles through leaves and branches from a clear blue sky, bracken was high on the slopes. Rupert, grimly hanging on, jolting along in the rear, heard Julie's confident voice – in the saddle she was assured, able to hold her own with anyone. And as a rider, indeed, she outclassed them all. From childhood days she had won prizes in local gymkhanas. More recently she had taken her place in county events, had even challenged some of the best-known men in the point-to-points. Rupert, watching her slim back as her mount cantered ahead, knew himself almost lost.

And as the days slid by, long days of high summer at Alnaker Hall, rose-pink walls centuries-old soaking up the sun as they'd done since Tudor times, leaded windows reflecting it with an apricot glow at sunset, velvet lawns stretching with green tranquillity down to the gentle slopes of the park and its spreading oaks, as the days grew longer and the nights shorter, Rupert knew himself quite lost, enraptured by Julie Alnaker and the Hall together.

Now, only three months later, crisp autumn days had come with wood smoke and a tang in the air, and they were to be married. The wedding was less than a week away.

Quite how it had come about Julie could not have said. Dazed by the whirl of events that summer, she looked back, tried to understand what had been going on. Rupert had been admiring from the beginning, of course, and her mother had always liked him. But at first, surely, she had had eyes only for Toby?

A lot of good that had done her. For after that one week-end, there had been no sign of him for another three weeks.

Rupert, though, had haunted the place. He had been there in any case during working hours, had often been invited by Veronica to stay on for dinner. He was extraordinarily attractive, too, and when he began to take her about, Julie had responded joyfully. Suddenly her days became fun. Finding herself in demand had been surprisingly pleasant. And her mother had smiled on them both. For Rupert was the sort of son-in-law she had hoped for. Presentable, attentive.

'Thank heavens,' she said to Miss Penrose – known always to the Alnakers as Rosie, and now Veronica's secretary, but once Julie's governess – 'we've seen no more of Toby Grant, since that week-end when Max would insist on inviting him to dinner and he monopolized Julie for hours.'

In fact, though, Toby had telephoned more than once, and during his rare off-duty he'd been out to the Hall, had hunted about for Julie. But on each occasion she'd been out, and the messages Toby left somehow lost themselves in the busy burcaucracy that was Alnaker Hall.

Finally her engagement to Rupert was announced. Not until then did Toby grasp how sure he had secretly been that she would be there, loyally waiting for him for ever if necessary. He had taken the news, as he took most of life's blows, on the chin. Facts were facts, and the past was gone. A future shared with Julie had, after all, been no more than a juvenile fantasy. Left with a sense of intolerable loneliness, he told himself firmly that he wanted her to be happy, went out to the Hall to give her his good wishes. He had to make several trips before he succeeded in catching up with her, and even then, hovering momentarily in the inner courtyard where they'd met, she had paused only briefly. 'Fittings,' she had gabbled, 'wedding arrangements, one mad whirl, you know, no time to stop now.'

He thought she'd put him off deliberately, but his father denied this, maintained Julie genuinely lacked a second to chat to anyone, was rushed off her feet. Overdoing it, he thought. There had been prolonged battles, too, he told Toby, with her mother over the wedding arrangements. The staff, watching the ebb and flow of these encounters, laid bets in the canteen as to who would emerge the victor, whether the marriage would be celebrated at home or in London. Veronica planned a vast society wedding with all the trimmings, and the picture she saw was St Margaret's, Westminster, Julie in a dress by Hartnell heavily encrusted with glitter, a long train to be carried by pages, six or eight bridesmaids – carefully matched, naturally, for height and colouring – and a reception at the Park Lane house for about five hundred. Or it might possibly have been five thousand. No one was exactly sure.

What Julie had seen was the village church at Alnaker St Nicholas across the park, a soft muslin dress with no train, no attendant either.

'I take it that's not what she's getting,' Toby commented wryly.

After weeks of skirmishing, Jo explained, and finally the intervention of Max Alnaker himself, a compromise satisfactory to neither party had been arranged. Julie would be married in the Cathedral at Halchester, there would be a special train from London, and Jo was to provide fleets of cars to ferry guests around the countryside throughout the day. The reception would be held at the Hall, and the dress would be

Mark Midwinter's version of the gown in the Gainsborough portrait of Emma Alnaker. The portrait had captured her at eighteen, in the charming gauzes of the day, ethereal, gay, her dark hair caught up in curls as casual as her hairdresser's skill could achieve, a fichu of fragile lace softening neck and shoulders, more lace flowing at the slender wrists. Midwinter had managed to update all this, yet retain its essence, the Gainsborough air of transparency. Even Veronica agreed Julie looked lovely in it, and Rosie was in raptures. 'A dream, Julie,' she breathed ecstatically. 'Out of this world.'

'Not quite, Rosie,' Veronica was compelled to point out, down to earth as ever. 'Hard cash is what we're paying for it, after all.'

As the Alnakers were commonly reputed to be among the richest families in the land, even Rosie was not thrown into too much agitation by this remark.

'But I must say,' Veronica continued fairly, 'although Mark's prices are so exorbitant, he does give value.' Veronica always liked to obtain value for money.

Julie hardly heard her. She was stunned. She had never believed she could look like this. The mirror told her she was going to be a beautiful bride, all dark hair, huge eyes, and the bewilderingly lovely dress.

Behind her Veronica was equally astonished. 'I have to hand it to you,' she admitted, surprise clearly evident. 'It was an inspiration to choose the dress in the portrait. I didn't think so at the time, but I ought to have realized what it would do for you. Incredible. Who could have supposed my funny little Julie would suddenly turn into a genuine beauty?'

Who, indeed?

Well, Toby for one, of course. But he was never to see her in the Gainsborough dress.

CHAPTER TWO

Hospital Call

'There's a call from the St John's Ambulance team at the point-to-point,' the registrar on duty that Saturday afternoon in the accident unit, Gavin Lowry, told Toby, unknowingly jerked him into nightmare. 'You'll have to go out there. One of the riders seems to have had a bad fall, and they don't want to move her until we've sent someone to have a look. They're afraid she may have a spinal injury, they say. So watch it.'

'She?' Toby repeated. Julie was riding in the point-to-point, he knew. Surely, though– 'Did you say *she?*' Could Julie be lying in some muddy field with a broken back?

Gavin caught the change in tone, looked up, surprised. 'They did say it was a girl, yes,' he agreed.

Toby was gone. Only the clatter of his feet to be heard as he ran through the hall, grabbed the accident bag from its cupboard by the entrance. The swing doors banged behind him, he hurled himself into the ambulance. As it howled along the High Street, over the traffic lights, finally turned into the lanes on the edge of the downs, he tried to tell himself not to be ridiculous. It couldn't be Julie.

But it was.

She was conscious, recognized him immediately, grinned at him in a panicky flicker. He knelt beside her. His hands were steady, gentle but assured. He examined her, talked to her, his voice quiet and confident. His feelings were different, could be read in his face all too easily. But no one was watching him. All eyes were on the patient.

The staff nurse who had come with him in the ambulance handed him the tailoring shears, always carried in the accident bag, and he slit Julie's jacket up the back, her shirt too. His fingers began probing. 'Pain?' he asked her.

Her cheek was pressed into the grass, her face covered in mud. 'No,' she said. 'No pain. It's just that I don't seem to be able to move at all.'

He went on with his examination.

Julie was mumbling disjointedly now, trying to tell him what had happened. 'I did what they say you should,' she began.

His fingers were exploring. He wanted to reject what they found.

'As we came down, I could see I...' Her voice died away momentarily, picked up again. 'I found myself going ... rolled up into a ball...'

He hated the results he was coming up with.

'On top of me, you know,' she said distinctly. 'Got kicked, I think ... bit of a muddle...' Her voice trailed away, she mumbled something he couldn't catch, but added in a rush: 'Toby, I'm so frightened. *Toby.*' One hand, up near her chin, moved convulsively, turned over and opened. 'Toby,' she said again.

He was thankful to see this much movement, at least, put his own hand round hers, clasped it securely, and wished that he could suppose calm and reassurance would at once, from his sure hold, sweep through her. First, though, he had to achieve the qualities himself. They seemed a long way off, a state of miserable anxiety much closer. But he was the man in charge, the one who had to see to it that nothing went wrong, that measures would be taken, survival be ensured. And damn it, he was going to see her all right. He'd been trained for it, and he could do it.

27

Confidence came to him then, and without hesitation he passed it on. 'All right, love. Not to worry. We're looking after you,' he said cheerfully. 'We've an ambulance here, and we're going to take you straight into St Mark's, see exactly what it is that's wrong. Probably you're mainly bruised, you know.' He wished he could believe it. 'Now I'm going to give you an injection, and then we'll be off.'

Comforted, she shut her eyes, her hand warmly in his. He felt sick again with fear. But the staff nurse had the syringe ready. He took it from her, concentrated firmly on the needs of the moment. The ambulance crew brought their stretcher up, with blankets, pillows, inflatable splints. He gave her the morphia, stood up. 'You're all right, Julie,' he told her. 'Just stay quietly there while the injection begins to work.' As if she could do anything else with an injury like that. His heart turned over and briefly, in that field on the hillside, a forlorn and cold desolation held him in its grip, as he glimpsed a bleak future.

'Now, a small conference,' he suggested briskly to the ambulance men, walked out of Julie's hearing. 'You were quite right,' he said to the St John's volunteers who had been

28

responsible for calling the accident unit. 'Undoubtedly she has a spinal injury. Very fortunate indeed you left her as she fell. Now, above all, we want to go very gently. Even the smallest movement could jar her spine, as you know, might increase the damage. The way we move her may make the difference between eventual recovery or paralysis.' He set his lips. Julie? Paralysed for the rest of her days? Not if he knew it. Not if anything he could do would prevent it. 'Her future may be in our hands *now*,' he told the ambulance crew. 'So I want her lifted on to the stretcher with no alteration in her position. No alteration whatsoever. And I mean exactly that. We'll need all of you to do it. Three of you to move her, to begin with, and the pillows and splints ready on the stretcher. We want to arrange them very carefully.' He began fiddling with them, glancing from them across to Julie, and back again. 'Once they're in position, they mustn't move either, as you set her down on them.'

The ambulance crew and the St John's men placed themselves and finally, like a well-trained, if unusually burly, corps de ballet moved in on the patient. They slipped a blanket under her, lifted her, face down, on to the stretcher. Cautiously across the bumpy field. Out through the gate. Slowly into the waiting ambulance.

'Good,' Toby said. 'Excellent.' Almost the exact opposite of what he was feeling.

At St Mark's Gavin Lowry met him, with the director of the accident unit. Simon Keeble was a highly competent young surgeon, who had trained at the unit in its early days under Adam Trowbridge himself. Today, as soon as he had the first report of this spinal injury, he had reached for the telephone. 'We'll get Trowbridge back,' he said to his registrar. Adam Trowbridge remained the unit's senior consultant still, came down from London weekly, and had been there that morning.

'He said he was going for a sail,' Gavin, always a worrier, warned him uneasily. 'He may not like–'

'Oh, he won't mind,' Simon said. 'At least, he may curse, probably will, but he'll always come when you call him.'

Half an hour later, Adam came striding in, a stocky square man, blunt-featured, with a pugnacious chin and a thinning cap of pale gold hair. They'd caught him at the sailing club – he kept his boat on a mooring outside the harbour, as he'd done for ten years now. They'd told him it was urgent, and he had not stopped to change, was in yellow sailing smock and trousers still, Dunlop boots, roll-neck sweater. With him into the hot-house atmosphere of the accident unit he brought a breath of fresh air, of the rugged outdoors. Simon Keeble, on the contrary, slim, with black hair and a sallow skin, was meticulous today in the dark formal suit he'd worn for Adam's clinic earlier. Registrars and house surgeons were white-coated, many of them dark-skinned, all of them worn, tired. Too little sleep, too little fresh air, too little exercise – other than what they gained pounding the wards and corridors of St Mark's – all these had taken their toll. The one girl among them, the Indian medical registrar, beautiful, a brilliantly flowered sari below her white coat, smiled wearily but encouragingly at the jittery Toby. At the best of times they were hopelessly overworked, and this was the week-end. Few ancillaries were on duty, and medical and nursing staff had to see to every technique needed.

Julie was the centre of their concern, a small slight figure huddled face down on the stretcher on which she'd been brought in, tubes winding snakelike round it now, glass bottles high and low. She was already in spinal shock. With damage to the spinal

31

cord, that was inevitable, would last for several days. But what they had to watch out for now was the sudden onset of circulatory shock, lowering her blood pressure, draining consciousness from her. This was the danger following any major injury, as in this unit they had all seen so often, when a patient could collapse and die in a few minutes. They had done what they could. Blood had been taken for grouping, a drip put up, blood pressure and heart-beat were monitored.

One of the Pakistani housemen brought in the X-rays from the radiology department. Adam looked at them. 'Well, as we expected,' he said. 'These don't tell us much more than we already know, do they?'

'We were afraid to pull her around at all,' Simon explained.

'Oh, I agree entirely. Much better wait until she's safely immobilized in plaster. Now there' – he pointed for the benefit of the assembled housemen – 'there's the fracture, of course. This lateral view does demonstrate it not too badly.' He peered at one picture after another, the registrars and housemen peered too, the talk became general.

'Now, about the position for plaster–'
'Hyperextension.'

'Got to be very careful, see the cord is not in danger of getting a new injury at the fracture site. You'll have to take another quick picture as you plaster, won't you, to make sure?' This was Adam again.

'Have her in a sling, would you say?'

'In as near natural position as we can get her, and then...'

The talk eddied and flowed. Snatches of it were to burn themselves into Toby's consciousness for ever.

'And what are we going to tell the parents?' Simon asked. 'They've been sent for – bound to be here soon.' He glanced at his watch. 'The prognosis isn't exactly hopeful, is it? But how much...?'

'All it would be advisable to say at this juncture, I should have thought, is...'

'Mainly a question of exactly how much involvement of the cord, isn't it?'

'Later on, of course, it will be possible to assess how much permanent damage there's going to be. In the meantime, though...'

The phrase reverberated down the corridors of Toby's mind. 'How much permanent damage ... how much permanent damage...'

Adam, talking to the housemen about the bone structure of the lower back, caught sight suddenly of his former house surgeon, and recognized his expression at once. He'd seen it a thousand times in the course of his working life, over a patient's bed in the wards, on the faces of relatives again and again. The agony of one who loved and despaired. 'You know this girl, Toby?' he broke off to ask.

Taken by surprise, Toby at first floundered. He swallowed, began again, achieved coherence. 'Yes, sir. I've known her all my life. Julie Alnaker. She – she was getting married next week.' He blurted this with increased desperation. His voice, he was afraid, was about to let him down, subject him to the unforgettable shame of crying like a child under the eyes of both consultants. As it was, Adam took in a great deal more than Toby suspected, though all he said was 'what appalling bad luck. Poor girl.'

The question of postponing the wedding was uppermost in Veronica's mind. 'Julie?' she had repeated, when Rosie first came to her with the news of the telephone call from St Marks. 'Julie's injured? Oh no, *not* in hospital, only four days before the wedding? Will she be out in time?'

Almost her first words to Simon and Adam, seeing her in the director's office at

34

the accident unit, were on this subject. 'But she's supposed to be married in the Cathedral on Wednesday.' The Rolls waiting outside, a mink coat thrown casually over her shoulders, her great eyes apparently accused them of deliberately plotting to sabotage this function.

That did it. Simon didn't know mink from musquash, but he could recognize egotism the minute he saw it. Veronica's attitude shocked him. He thought of the patient they'd left in the intensive care ward, the long hard road she had to travel before she could achieve any sort of health or mobility, and made no attempt whatever to disguise his disapproval of this incredibly silly woman and her irrelevant chatter about the Cathedral and a wedding next week.

'You don't seem to understand,' he said coldly. 'Your daughter will be in the ward here next week. And for many weeks after that.' He glared coldly.

Veronica, who was used these days to an almost excessive amount of consideration, not to mention adulation, from everyone round her, was shattered. She was, after all, the patient's mother, wasn't she? Surely she was entitled to sympathy? This callous behaviour was monstrous. One thing was certain. She was not going to stand by and see Julie abandoned to the unfeeling care of this impossible man. She began at once to inquire about the possibility of transferring her daughter to a private room, obtaining a second opinion without delay.

Both Adam and Simon regarded her with exasperated frustration. Had she understood nothing of what they had tried to tell her?

At this point, to everyone's enormous relief, Max arrived. He knew Adam already, was thankful to see him there. 'I was going to try to get hold of you,' he greeted him. 'But here you are, before me. Splendid. Tell me, how's my daughter?'

'In no immediate danger now.' Adam's response was quick, for here, it was apparent to all of them, was a very worried man. 'But she does have this spinal injury, I'm afraid, and any damage to the spinal cord is always a tricky business.'

'Tricky?' Max repeated.

'I'm afraid so. With an injury like this, the trouble is always that it's not the fracture of the bone that presents the real danger. That would be comparatively simple to deal with – though I'm afraid, Lord Alnaker, even then she would still be immobilized for the next few weeks. As it is, she'll have to remain flat, and in plaster, for months. The spinal cord, you see, functions rather like an enormous telephone cable. It carries all the lines of communication for the body, conducts messages up and down from the brain. And without these messages there can be no activity. No movement, no sensation.'

'So what you're telling me, then, is that this cable, the spinal cord, has been damaged?' Max asked.

'That's what we'd like to know. We can't say for sure yet. Certainly the cord is out of action at the moment, but then this is to be expected. It's due to the bone fracture, and may not last. Because it's so vital, you see, the cord is extraordinarily well protected, in the equivalent of an armoured case. This case is what's been injured. The bony covering has been broken, fractured, low down in her back. Here.' He turned and demonstrated the X-ray, in the viewing box on Simon's desk. 'She has what's called a fracture-dislocation there.' He pointed with his pen at the faint line, to Max indistinguishable from all the other blurs and shadows on the picture. He stared hopelessly at it, said nothing.

'What we can't tell yet,' Adam went on, 'is if the message-carrying cable has been interrupted. It's gone out of action, as I said, but that's always to be expected in this type of injury, may be only for a matter of days. And unfortunately X-rays can't tell us a thing about this. They don't show the cord, you see, only its bony covering.' His pen ran along the line of the spinal column in the X-ray. 'So although we can see the break in the bone, here, we can't tell what's happened to the cord inside.'

'So what's next?' Max asked.

'The only way to find out – we have no means of actually examining the cord, I'm afraid – is by watching it function. Seeing what it can do, whether it carries on as it used to, or not. Whether the messages get through, in fact.'

Max nodded.

'But at present, spinal shock has set in, and it's not working at all. So there's nothing for us to observe, and in that respect we're at a standstill. When spinal shock wears off, though, the cord may be in full working order. Or it may not.' The words fell ominously.

'If it isn't, what then?'

'Then we have to find out how much of it is working, which we can only do by seeing exactly what messages do get through. This is when we have to enlist the help of the neurologists, who have a much more detailed understanding than the rest of us of the intricacies of the nerve pathways. But all this may be a very slow business, I'm afraid, especially as some messages that can't get along the original pathway may, in the course of time, find a new route for themselves. So at this stage, as we were explaining to Lady Alnaker, it's quite impossible to know how much permanent damage there's going to be.'

'When you talk of permanent damage,' Max said, 'what exactly do you mean?'

'I mean some sort of paralysis,' Adam said bluntly. 'Possibly for years. Even possibly, I have to warn you frankly, for the remainder of her life. We must all hope, of course, that this is an unduly pessimistic forecast, but things could be as bad as that.'

Julie lay now in the intensive care ward, pale as the plaster encasing her. Rupert, by her side, was in despair.

This hospital revolted him. The ventilators, oscilloscopes, tubes and apparatus everywhere. The busy preoccupied staff, in crisp uniforms or white coats, intent on their own concerns and seemingly so self-assured, in sharp contrast to the patients, who were almost naked, lost, vulnerable, the playthings of buzzers and flashing lights, machinery that clicked and hummed and had its way with them.

He took refuge, as he sat there, in the memory of their past happiness, told himself that one day they'd regain it, vowed it should not have vanished for ever, snatched away as Julie twisted and fell at that jump on the edge of the downs. He thought longingly of that first week-end he'd been at the Hall, when Julie had been so gay and lovely, and they'd danced all night in the gallery. He'd first lost his heart to her then. The week-end, later, when he'd finally taken his courage in both hands and proposed. That had been after the *Son et Lumière*. The setting of the rose-pink walls, the terrace and the night sky, the pageantry and poetry, had been inexpressively moving, but Julie's guitar playing had lifted him out of himself, had touched him at some deep level – a level that he'd hardly known he'd possessed until then. His feeling for her, already almost beyond his control, had suddenly overwhelmed him. Watching her, so quietly beautiful, so much a part of the history of her home, so lovely, so fragile, her long fingers producing chords that would echo and vibrate through his soul for ever, he had wanted only to be allowed to love her all the days of her life.

Yet this was what it had come to, the happiness and hope. To this intensive care ward, where immobilized, drugged, a frail broken body in plaster, all her bodily needs seen to by the nursing staff, she was beyond his reach. Nothing he could do would make any difference to her condition. She wasn't even aware he was with her.

He didn't know how to bear it.

He found, though, that he didn't have to. As soon as the night staff came on, a sister spoke to him, advised him to have a meal. 'But if I were you, I'd go and have a good night's sleep,' she urged him kindly.

'At the moment, the patient doesn't really know whether you're here or not. You'd do much better to go home. We'll ring you if there's any change. When she's fully conscious again, she'll need you with her. Not now.'

Excellent advice, he thought, and he took it. In an effort to quieten his tumbling thoughts, the pictures that crowded his mind, he walked the four miles out to the Hall. Through the darkening streets of the old cathedral city, and out along the narrow winding lanes, smelling of grass and leaf

41

mould, wood smoke from the cottages, and the chrysanthemums and dahlias that in daylight glowed like jewels in their gardens. Time would pass, he told himself. Surely, the day would come when he would hold Julie in his arms again, free from the plaster, the tubing, all the hideous apparatus that had taken her from him, made her its own.

At the Hall he was jolted into reality. All was bustle, telephoning, conferences. Inside five minutes he was sitting in Veronica's office, a list in his hand and a telephone at his elbow.

Max himself was not to be seen. He had informed Veronica crisply that nothing need be done about the wedding until Monday, when two good girls from an agency could see to it. He had then gone off on his own and shut himself into his study, refusing to speak to anyone.

Rupert, though, was thankful for the distraction of the lists and the telephone. Thankful, too, to be able to help Veronica.

She was, in her own eyes at least, rising magnificently to the crisis. Luckily for her, she had very little imagination, was saved as a result from the anxiety Max was enduring. No terrifying possibilities – pneumonia, infection, and – what was it Adam had mentioned? – ascending oedema of the cord, or simply sudden fatal shock – none of these dangers presented themselves repeatedly to Veronica's inward eye. She lived firmly in the present – where, as she pointed out somewhat tartly, there was a great deal that needed doing. Today's problems were quite enough to be going on with. Her greatest anxiety remained the wedding, and was centred almost wholly on the necessity of preventing hordes of people arriving for a non-event. Her secret dread was a cathedral full of wedding guests and no bride. This hideous outcome preoccupied her to the exclusion of everything else. She felt, to be honest, a little like an impresario whose leading lady has let him down just before opening night. Most unfortunately, too, brides having no understudies, operation cancellation had to be mounted.

At breakfast on Sunday she allocated duties confidently, was surprised, a little put out, when Rupert explained apologetically that he might not be available. He was hoping to go to St Mark's to see Julie.

'Oh,' she said blankly. 'But Max will be seeing to all that. Won't you, darling?'

Max suggested mildly that Julie might perhaps like to have Rupert with her.

Veronica turned her wide gaze on him again. 'Oh,' she said. 'Yes, I suppose so.' She could almost be seen reversing switches in her head, diverting Rupert back from the role of personal assistant to that of prospective bridegroom. 'If she wants him to, of course he must,' she added more definitely.

Rupert thought he'd telephone the hospital immediately after breakfast.

'Good,' Veronica agreed. 'That's one thing dealt with. I won't bother.' She crossed through an item in her notebook, and her eyes caught by the next entry, turned to Miss Penrose. 'Look, Rosie,' she began, 'we must make sure to inform the florist's in good time. There'll be no one there today, of course. But we mustn't forget. Then there's the cake. I wonder what we'd better do about the cake? Max, what do *you* think we ought to do about the cake? Should we offer it to the old people's home, or keep it for the estate party at Christmas?'

With all this going on, Rupert began to feel more optimistic. Veronica had succeeded in domesticating tragedy, and his fearful forebodings receded. He helped himself to more coffee and another piece of toast. If he could be of any assistance, he told her, he could, after all, simply pop down to the hospital for an hour this morning, and perhaps again this afternoon. The rest of the day he could be available.

'Oh, Rupert, how very thoughtful of you!' she exclaimed. 'I don't know what I'd do without you.'

Fully restored, he went off to telephone.

Max followed him. 'I want to hear what they've got to say. We can make the call from my office.'

This unnerved Rupert. He'd always been in awe of Julie's father, and to have a complicated conversation with some unknown doctor about her, with Max breathing down his neck, nonplussed him. However, Max himself rescued him from this anxiety. 'We'd better talk to young Toby,' he announced. 'Trowbridge told me he'd be looking after Julie.' He picked up the telephone, asked the switchboard for the hospital. 'Mind if I have a word with him first?'

Rupert assured him he'd be only too glad.

'Good. Great lad, our Toby,' Max remarked absently, his eyes far away. 'You met him, of course.'

St Mark's answered.

Max was peremptory. Unaware that his attitude was in any way out of the ordinary, 'Lord Alnaker,' he said. 'I want Toby Grant.'

CHAPTER THREE

Intensive Care

Toby had had no sleep that night. No night staff had ordered him out of the unit. On the contrary, rushed off their feet, they had been thankful to discover that one of the housemen at least looked like remaining there to help them out.

His feelings were a chaos. Misery, pain and anxiety struggled to have their way with him. But six years of training held, enabled him to ignore his own reactions, get on with the job. Brain and hands functioned normally, though terror for Julie hovered, tried more than once to take over. One fact he was sure of – too late, of course – she should have been marrying him, not Rupert. But as resolutely as he had once denied the strength of his own feelings, he now pushed aside this useless piece of knowledge. For he had watched Rupert at Julie's bedside, had seen for himself that there could be no doubt of his love for her. He had been in agony. And after all it was Rupert Julie had promised to marry, Rupert she had chosen. Only as a patient, Toby had to remind himself, was she any concern of his. His place was to look after her physical needs, to keep his head clear and his mind alert. And that illicit intruder, his love for her trampled underfoot.

In the few quiet moments that the night offered, though, Toby – like Rupert – found his mind travelling back into a past when hope and joy had beckoned still, until almost deliberately he had thrown them away, on the evening of the *Son et Lumière*, when they had had their disastrous quarrel.

Of course, Toby had always disliked the recurrent hullabaloo that these days was dignified by the designation of the *Son et Lumière*. Originally it had simply been known as the Alnaker St Nicholas village pageant, and as children both he and Julie had been unwilling participants. Over the years Veronica had worked indefatigably on it, until eventually, by altering the time to late evening, adding, with the inspiration she could occasionally produce, stanzas of poetry and song, snatches of music, fractured history – gorgeously costumed if wildly inaccurate – she had made it at last into a notable spectacle. The audience came from far and wide, paid hard cash (to the Commonwealth Fund for Famine Relief) to hear thrilling voices declaim poetry against the floodlit background of the lovely Tudor buildings, music fill the air. A magical evening, and these days almost guaranteed to go without a hitch, too, as none of the actors were allowed to have any lines they might ruin. Veronica had arranged for the entire production to be pre-recorded with professional voices. The cast was required only to sweep about on the terrace under the spotlights, magnificently apparelled and concentrate on their timing and positioning. Rehearsal after rehearsal, Veronica's undoubted bullying, and the lavish use of coloured chalk, saw to this.

To cover the intervals while the cast changed their superb costumes, Julie went on to the terrace, the spotlight found her, she sang old English ballads – selected by Veronica – and accompanied herself with chords from her guitar. At first, petrified, she had tried anxiously to argue herself out of the horrifying duty. But Veronica, as so often, had been adamant.

Toby knew perfectly well that Julie always dreaded her entrance. He remembered too, how, when he came upon her, waiting in the orangery with her guitar, she looked so unbearably lovely that he had caught his breath in wonder. Why in the world hadn't he simply told her how beautiful she was, how much he loved her?

Instead he'd lashed out blindly. The truth was, he'd thought only of himself. By then, he'd heard about Rupert. Consumed with jealousy, he'd panicked and hit out. Seeing her so poised and worldly, too, he had understood what they all meant. They warned him she was Lord Alnaker's daughter, from high society, not for him. In the orangery she had let the long black velvet cloak, lined with white ermine, slip from her bare shoulders. White chiffon floated in subtle – and expensive, even he could see that – pleats to her toes, which he glimpsed through a mesh of gold thronging. In her hair, piled high on her head, a diamond comb, a diamond bracelet on her wrist. The diamonds, of course, were Veronica's. Toby knew this as well as anyone. But the knowledge served only to increase his sense of alienation. At that moment she seemed to him wholly her mother's daughter.

He had told her so, in no complimentary manner, and they had begun arguing furiously. Meanwhile, as they were at it, the entire cast surged, like some Elizabethan mob, through the orangery towards the dressing rooms. It was the first interval. Julie broke off in mid-sentence, pulled her cloak up round her shoulders, took her guitar and, head in the air, left him, stepped out on to the terrace, began to play.

Away from him for ever, he thought now. And all his own doing. Even that same evening he had longed to call his embittered words back. Too late, though.

He knew he would never have spoken so harshly had he not loved her so much. But how was she supposed to guess this? It certainly hadn't been apparent from the words he'd chosen. And what a moment he'd picked for delivering his unwelcome truths (for truths they had been, this he continued to believe), assaulting her with them when she was already keyed up, ready to go on to the terrace and perform before the assembled public, waiting out there in the dusk. And what was it, in any case, that had made him want to destroy her self-confidence so brutally?

In the event, he had been the one to suffer, for Julie had gone on alone, into her own world, another relationship, her future marriage. He had forced her into this. And, he had to admit, there seemed no reason to assume that she would not be a great deal better off with Rupert than she would have been with him. What sort of husband would he make her – given to these bouts of consuming jealousy, to abusing her simply because she looked beautiful and happened to be wearing her mother's diamonds? No doubt Rupert could easily do better than this. He almost certainly loved her as much, was far more even-tempered into the bargain.

With the petulant hand of an irritable child, Toby thought, he'd thrown his own future away. If he had to pay the price for the rest of his days, it served him damn well right. Now all he could do for Julie was see to her physical needs, try to ensure her survival from this dangerous injury. And keep his emotions to himself. No quarrelling, at least. No loving, either.

Morning came, and Max was on his way with Rupert. Toby went out into the corridor to meet them. He'd been on his feet for twenty-four hours. It might have been a week.

His appearance alarmed Max as nothing else had done. He had never expected to see Toby, of all people, so haggard, worn, defeated. Were things much worse than he had supposed? For Toby to look like this, they must be. 'Not dying, is she, Toby?' he blurted out.

Toby had never foreseen that the day would come when he found himself reassuring Max Alnaker. 'No, no, sir. She's quite reasonably comfortable. No cause for alarm.' He shoved the horrors that had been haunting him all night out his mind. 'She's all right. Come in and see her.' He raised a cheerful smile.

Max smiled too. 'You're amazingly like your father sometimes, Toby,' he said. 'A great standby.' He patted him on the shoulder – he had to reach upwards to do it, but neither of them noticed this. 'Thank you, lad. I can't tell you what a comfort it is to know you're here with her.'

Toby took him into the ward.

Afterwards he went down to the car park with him, saw he'd brought the Land-Rover, was driving himself.

'Got to keep a date with your father now,' Max told him. 'We're both a bit uneasy about the security system. It's the pictures, you see. That great crowd we had in a few months back raised all sorts of disturbing queries in both our minds. Your father thinks we ought to have more men on patrol, a better alarm system too, these lawless days. Sometimes I wonder if – ah well, never

52

mind, not your worry. If it isn't one thing it's another, eh? About Julie, Toby – you won't hesitate to ring me, will you, if there's any change, anything I ought to know about? Wherever I am. Home or abroad. And insist on speaking to me personally, won't you? Whatever they may try to tell you.'

Toby assured him he would, almost patted him back on the broad shoulder hunched now over the driving wheel. 'Don't worry. I'll keep in touch. And I'll get through all right, too. They won't stop me.'

'No. I don't suppose they will,' Max agreed, a glint in his eye. 'Shan't tell Jo how whacked you look, though. Can't afford to have two worried fathers around the place. Get a rest, though, won't you, as soon as you can?'

'House surgeons don't sleep,' Toby said with a grin. 'It's well known. Or only on their feet. Don't you worry too much about Julie, sir. With any reasonable luck, it should simply be a question of time and care now.' Rupert's time, his care, he thought miserably.

Tired and edgy, he went back to the intensive care ward, found sister in one of her moods. She had discovered Rupert, she announced, ploughing remorselessly through the details involved in cancelling Miss

53

Alnaker's wedding. So she had taken it on herself, she said, to throw the young man out. She didn't suppose Lord Alnaker would be exactly pleased to hear it, but that would be just too bad, as far as she was concerned. 'Over my dead body,' she informed Toby in ringing tones, 'will I have that Mr Ferris back in my ward for more than five minutes at a stretch. Of all the inconsiderate thoughtless...' She continued in this strain, released a vast amount of pent-up irritation. Toby, she was gratified to find, swung at once into a raging fury that outdid even her own bad temper, and the two of them spent a splendid ten minutes demolishing Rupert's character in detail.

That afternoon, when he reappeared, somewhat timidly and with a cautious eye cocked towards sister's office, it was Toby who descended on him like the wrath of God, told him exactly where he had gone wrong in the ward that morning.

Rupert snapped back vehemently, as he had not dared to do with sister. He was blowed if he would be spoken to like this by any young pipsqueak of a junior doctor from nowhere, years younger than he was, newly qualified. Who did he think he was?

Afterwards, though, sitting guiltily beside

a drugged and sleeping Julie, he was ashamed, recognized he'd been mistaken. He had wanted Julie to know what was happening at the Hall, not to feel cut off from all the action he had been taking on her behalf. No more than that. But it had been a bad time to choose, he could see that now. He watched her anxiously, blamed himself for his thoughtlessness.

Even so, rightly or wrongly, he couldn't quite find it in him to overlook Toby's behaviour, began to seek opportunities to cut that self-satisfied young house surgeon down to size.

To Julie, it seemed whenever she swam up out of the fuzziness in which she was submerged, there were two faces hovering in the air above. Two cross, angry faces. Toby and Rupert.

As her head cleared, pain took over. Her bruised and battered body screamed for attention. They drugged her less now, told her she should be thankful for these agonies. The pain meant, they assured her, that her spinal cord was still partly functioning. 'Can you feel this?' they inquired daily. 'And this? Or this?' With any luck, they informed her, one day she'd be able to walk again, though they warned her, of course, it might be only with two sticks and her legs in irons. They appeared to imagine this made something to look forward to. Only continuous pain, aching misery, knives that stabbed without warning, turned fiercely in her bones. Unless drugged almost to insensibility, she could find no comfort. She was ashamed of her lack of fortitude. Other people, she was sure, did better than this. She longed to be self-controlled, courageous. Instead she had to recognize that she was tearful, jumpy, frightened, waiting for the next bout of pain. Impatient and irritable, too. She complained, she knew, often, sounded to herself like a whining child. A cowardly, disagreeable, whining child, a nuisance to everyone.

'Are they all very fed up with me?' she asked Toby. 'Am I being an impossible patient?' She'd receive the truth from him, if from no one else.

'No more than most,' he said, grinned cheerfully. He had been taking her blood pressure. 'When you're ill, duckie, you're ill. We're used to people in pain here, you know. No stiff upper lip is demanded. Or expected.' He bent down, did something to the bed, something else to the pillows at her knees. She at once felt an amazing relief, as strains and pressures lifted, and existence

56

became bearable again. 'Have a drink of this,' he suggested, held her head with one hand, the feeding cup with the other. 'Better soon, love. A little sleep now, eh?'

She drifted off to sleep, a sense of total security enveloping her.

'I ought to try not to be such a cry-baby,' she muttered apologetically a day or two later, after a tough session with the neurologist and his registrar. She longed for Toby's reassurance.

'Oh yes,' he agreed. 'You must keep on trying. You mustn't ever give up. If we're to have you back on your feet, you've got to fight all the way.'

She hardly took in what he said. 'I get so tired of trying not to howl,' she told him. 'I can just about manage it when strangers are here, but then I go to pieces afterwards.'

He took her hand in one of his. 'Bellow away, sweetheart,' he encouraged her with a lightness she believed in, though he didn't for a moment deceive himself. 'It's only us, you know, and we're all used to it here. Do you good to unload occasionally.'

Unexpectedly she turned her head into his hand, pushed suddenly like a small animal in pain, or an anguished child, and began to sob softly. The sound tore Toby apart. He put a hand round her limp tousled curls, wet with sweat, held her firmly, glad that she couldn't see his face. Hands and voice he might be able to control, but his face gave him away.

For these lonely moments of comfort and tenderness – not the first or the last he offered her – he had to pay a price. His own total commitment to her. He loved her now more deeply than ever before. This, though, he was determined she should never discover. He was there as a doctor, to offer his skill and care in her treatment, all that he had learnt at medical school and on the wards at the Central. Friendship could go along with this, friendship and loving-kindness, reassurance and compassion. No more.

Rupert continued to come in daily. Continued, too, to bring with him Veronica's worries and queries, and, more recently, a pile of letters to be signed. For Veronica had engaged the two good girls from the agency that Max had recommended, and had cleared, with the additional assistance of Rupert and Rosie, the immediate problems of cancelling both wedding and reception. After this had been achieved, one of the agency girls returned to London, but the other, Samantha Marston, a beautiful and highly efficient blonde, remained. She was now ploughing through a vast number of letters in response to the inquiries that poured in asking about Julie's health. Samantha devised a basic reply to these, which she typed out, and Rupert brought in to Julie at the rate of about half a dozen each day. Julie had to add some sort of personal message to every letter and her signature.

Sister complained again to Toby. 'That wretched fiancé of Miss Alnaker's expects too much.'

'He's very attentive,' Toby pointed out, this being the point that had stuck him most. 'Comes in every day.'

'Upsets her every day too. Wears her out. All those unnecessary problems and details, and those letters he keeps bringing her to sign. Surely, with that enormous staff at Alnaker Hall, someone else could see to them?'

'They don't seem to think so, do they?' Toby asked. 'And I'm not sure it's altogether a bad thing, either, sister,' he added conscientiously. 'Keeps her in touch with what's going on at home, sees that she's alert and involved.'

'It tires her out,' sister repeated. 'But of course if you think it's all right, I suppose it's no good me trying to put a stop to it.'

Toby had his doubts about this.

'As long as you don't feel it's holding her back,' sister ended ominously.

As she demonstrated every intention of repeating this conversation twice daily, Toby decided to mention the problem to Gavin Lowry.

The registrar shrugged. 'If we stop her fiancé coming in she'll be upset, on the other hand if we let him in he upsets her and tires her out. On the whole I'm in favour of him doing the upsetting. In any case, it's perfectly normal for a girl to be a bit up and down when her fiancé comes to see her. Especially this girl – after all, she was on the point of marrying the bloke when this disaster struck, wasn't she? I don't honestly think it's for us to protect her from the stress of dealing with this. She's going to live with him, it's up to her to come to terms with him the way he is.'

'That's what I thought,' Toby agreed, though he found this conversation rather more unsettling than those he had with sister. How pleasant it would have been if Gavin had taken a strong attitude, forbidden Rupert more than five minutes a day with Julie, as sister had done in the early stages. 'Sister,' he said, 'maintains it's interfering with her recovery.'

Gavin smiled. 'Naturally,' he said. 'We all know sister thinks recovery would progress much more smoothly if only families could be prevented from continually bursting in with their untidy and disruptive emotions.'

What they none of them knew was that Julie was facing a very specific problem over Rupert's daily visits. For these had become no more than an unwanted interruption to some sort of hidden dialogue going on between herself and Toby. 'Falling in love with your doctor, that's what you're doing, my girl,' she admonished herself with increasing frequency. 'Patients are always doing it. It's a well-known phenomenon, and means nothing.'

But still she searched for his arrival in the ward, watched his every action. Toby, in a white coat, fair haired and bony, rather untidy, often frowning, his blue eyes remote, concentrated, as he adjusted the apparatus surrounding her, or took her blood pressure. Her heart turned over with the sheer joy of having him there at her side.

Toby, puzzled, took a second reading.

Unfortunately, though, her heart had quite ceased to turn over when Rupert sat by her side, rustling letters and lists, or recounting the progress of the alternations to the west wing at the Hall and the plans for the cottages down by the Hard. But, she reminded herself sternly, it was Rupert she had promised to marry – nearly had married. He had once made her happier than she'd ever been.

Now, though, he was simply an interruption. All day long she kept watching for Toby, hungered for the sound of his voice in the ward. When he was there, radiance filled her with hope and expectation. The pain, the constant physical misery, the tears, the restless discomfort, the shame of having to be looked after like a baby, potted and cleaned and turned – all this became bearable. Because Toby was around, her life had meaning, the air glittered with promise. He had only to stand in the unit, talking to sister, doing a round with Gavin Lowry, or seeing to a new admission, and she watched him as if, she told herself furiously, he was a pop star newly arrived in London Airport and she an ecstatic teeny bopper.

A momentary madness only, she decided daily – hourly, even. Some sort of institutional hysteria had taken hold of her. As soon as she left the hospital, the mood would evaporate, vanish completely, life would return to normality. And a good thing too. What she was experiencing was nothing other than an immature, adolescent reaction towards authority in a white coat. The sooner she went home and forgot it the better.

Veronica achieved this ambition for her. As soon as Julie was pronounced to be out of danger, Veronica began a campaign to move her from St Mark's, which she appeared to regard as an out-moded poor-low institution left over from Queen Victoria's day. Only the united efforts of Max Alnaker, Adam Trowbridge and Simon Keeble had kept Julie there for the first four weeks of the three-month period she had to remain in bed. After that, though, Max had been forced to agree that an agency would undoubtedly be able to supply capable and experienced nurses to care for Julie at home. Simon Keeble was entirely in favour of ridding himself of Veronica's regular presence and interference in the running of his unit, while Adam Trowbridge had to admit he could keep in touch with Julie at Alnaker Hall almost as easily as he had been doing at St Mark's.

'But if you think there's any danger at all in the move,' Max said, 'I'll put my foot down hard and she'll stay where she is.'

'Not to say danger, no,' Adam said slowly. 'What then?'

Adam shook his head. 'It's all a bit intangible, I'm afraid. Difficult to pin down. But patients often tend to do better when they're surrounded by others in the same boat. Like having the stimulus of competition at school – even the best tutors produce quite a different effect, don't they? And private nursing could be surprisingly similar to the best tutors. On the other hand, Julie would certainly be much more comfortable at home. And she can't stay in the intensive care ward, either, for the full three months. So in any case, she'll have to be moved. Either home, or perhaps to the regional spinal centre. And I must say it does seem unkind to insist that she has a tough time in a ward full of spinal cases, when she could be cared for most adequately in the comfort of her own home. So suppose we try her there for the next couple of months, say, then we can think again, see how much progress she's made. A short break from institutional routine will probably do her nothing but good.'

So at the end of the week Julie went home. Three nursing sisters and Rosie were to look after her in the Gatehouse.

For his part, Toby tried to forgot that he had once had a personal life he had dreamed of sharing with her. For a young house surgeon, of course, there was less difficulty about this than there would have been for most young men. The problem for junior hospital doctors had always been to attempt to reserve any time at all for personal concerns. Easy, too, for Toby to tell himself he had no opportunity to go out to the Hall to discover how Julie was settling down. It happened to be no more than the truth.

Only two weeks later, in any case, his appointment at St Mark's came to an end, and he returned to the Central London Hospital. The best cure for him, he reminded himself, was to stay away.

In some respects it would even be a relief to do this. Throughout her stay in the unit, while he had been caring for her, he had been in conflict, at odds with himself, fighting his own feelings. Now he could settle down to work, leave Julie to settle down to a future with Rupert. He scowled, and slammed doors behind him.

CHAPTER FOUR

The Gatehouse

Veronica had enjoyed planning Julie's return home to the Gatehouse. There had been a great deal to do, of course. Nursing staff had to be engaged and housed, for one thing, though housing them at the Hall presented no real difficulty, merely the exercise of administrative judgement. Five years earlier the East wing had been made over for staff use entirely, converted into bed-sitting rooms and flats, extra bathrooms put in, an ironing room installed, a hairdressing salon opened, common rooms and a canteen added. New kitchens had been built, to serve not only the canteen but the family dining room in the centre block. When these alterations had been completed, the architects, Armitage and Waldron – Rupert's firm – had turned their attention to the Gatehouse. The original plan had been to convert this to a private residence for Julie's brother James, the Alnaker's only son and heir. Two years Julie's senior, he had been in his final term at Eton when the conversion had been started, had been expected to go on to Oxford and read classics. Instead, though, he had suddenly abandoned Oxford and his family, had left their high hopes for him shattered, had departed for Nepal in a Land-Rover with a group of friends, had not been seen since, though the expedition had set off four years earlier. 'My drop-out son, believed to be somewhere in India or points eastwards,' Max referred to him ruefully.

Veronica had been stunned when he left, continued to miss him, she told her friends, every day of her life. Her only son, and she had adored him. No one dared to say that James might have found her adoration smothering, claustrophobic, had left for Nepal to escape her influence. Max, who loved both of them, knew, but he said nothing.

It had been Max, though, who had insisted, when Julie left school, that the Gatehouse, now empty and ready for occupation – two floors, a large living room and kitchen on the first floor, two bedrooms and a bathroom above – should be decorated and furnished for her.

Her return to it now, Veronica realized,

might provide a solution to one problem that had been bothering her for some weeks. The problem of Rosie. For the employment of the two agency secretaries had brought home to Veronica exactly how shockingly muddled and slow poor old Rosie had become.

In fact, Julie could have told her mother this years earlier. When she had first left school she had planned to go on to university – she had three A-levels. Veronica, though, pressed her to live at home, act as her secretary. She had lost one of her children, was determined to hang on to the other at all costs. That the costs might have to be paid by the child rather than by herself failed to enter into her calculations, in all probability would have failed to deter her if it had.

Max, however, had seen trouble coming, had warned Julie that the plan would never work. 'Your mother,' he told her bluntly, 'genuinely does need some help. But to be quite honest – much better to face this in advance – she'll only accept it from you so long as you do what she says, and no questions asked. Frankly, my dear, I don't see this happening. You keep out of it, let her engage a good secretary from London. Then, if they don't get on, they can always part and no harm done. You go up to university and improve your mind.' He had smiled encouragingly. 'You've got one, you know. So how about using it, eh?'

But his advice had fallen on deaf ears. Elated to see Veronica valued her assistance, Julie – longing, too, to play her part in the running of the Hall – ignored Max's advice, took a secretarial course in Halchester, and returned home to pull her weight and eventually become, as she imagined, something like her mother's partner.

She soon discovered that Max had been right. Veronica was not looking for any sort of partner, not even for an assistant. Only for a slave. What neither of them had expected, though, was that Rosie would complicate the situation even further.

Rosie interfered in everything Julie tried to carry out, bossed her and criticized her – in a kindly but immensely disparaging manner – all her efforts. Julie, who was, after all, totally ignorant of office procedure outside the secretarial college, felt bound to accept Rosie's instructions as to 'the way *we* do things here'. All too soon she found that, far from acting as Veronica's partner, she had degenerated into merely Rosie's shorthand typist. It was Rosie who discussed plans and projects, appointments and hospitality with

Veronica, passed on the details – muddled and impractical – to Julie, dictated pathetically verbose, involved letters for Julie to type and Veronica to sign.

Julie's hands were tied. She was far too fond of both participants in this unrewarding, woman-made shambles to try to opt out of it. Veronica was maddening, of course, but she had only recently lost James. Julie knew the hurt went deep, couldn't bring herself to establish a family pattern of walking out on Veronica. Then there was Rosie.

Julie loved Rosie. Throughout her childhood – Rosie had first come to the Hall as a nursery governess when Julie had been only three – Rosie had been there, infinitely closer to her than the awe-inspiring and distant Veronica. Because of this, though often infuriated by her, Julie had a strong protective urge to cover up her incompetence, hold her job down for her. Finally she had simply written off her first plans as a dead loss, resigned herself to helping Rosie out in the office, doing the typing and the filing, and then escaping into the woods and moors, or losing herself in the picture gallery and the library. Time slipped by, the years formed an undemanding sequence. More and more she suspected that she ought to break away.

Then Rupert had come, provided an escape, put a stop to all planning except for marriage.

Even so, Julie had done far more in the secretarial field than Veronica had ever given her credit for, and with Julie in hospital, Rosie stood out in all her garrulous incompetence, muddled, and slow as a wet week. Veronica was looking for an excuse to engage Samantha permanently – the girl was not only enormously capable, but charming, too. Above all, fast.

But Veronica was fond of Rosie, in her own way, certainly didn't want to upset her. Inspiration came. Rosie must look after Julie.

'I don't know, Rosie darling, how I shall possibly manage without you.' Veronica adopted a convincing air of martyrdom. 'But Julie must come first with both of us. If you are looking after her I shall be able to be easy in my mind, because of course I always know I can trust you utterly. I wouldn't think of leaving her in the hands of any agency nurse, however well qualified they said she was. But with you there I shan't need to worry. So I shall simply have to keep Samantha on, and let you give all your time to Julie.'

This line worked. Secretly Rosie had been alarmed to discover the most incredible standard of speech and efficiency Samantha displayed, had felt her own position increasingly menaced. Now, though, she could abandon the struggle to keep up, could turn to Julie instead. She fussed over her like a hen with one chick, in a manner the nursing sisters considered ridiculous. To Julie herself, though, all Rosie's cherishing and fussing came as a pleasant change from the rigours of St Mark's. The food at home, too, was a relief after hospital catering.

Dr Buckland, the Alnakers' family doctor, came in every day and cosseted her. Getting on for seventy now, he had looked after the Alnakers for almost half a century, had seen Julie through measles and chicken pox, concussion once, a broken ankle once, a sprained wrist twice, numerous minor upsets and head colds. Now he intended to see her as comfortably as possible through the prolonged after-effects of this major injury. She had a long hard haul ahead of her, he knew, a great deal of inevitable pain to endure. Anything he could do to help her, he was prepared to undertake. He and Rosie conferred, agreed on their policy. Everything must be made easy for Julie.

Adam Trowbridge had ordered daily physiotherapy, passive exercises at first only, of course, and Dr Buckland engaged a private physiotherapist, Miss Makepeace, who lived locally, to come in each morning. Under Dr Buckland's guidance, everyone was gentle and understanding with Julie, no one attempted to force her into any activity before she was sure she was ready for it. The new régime could hardly have been more different from the accident unit, where the staff had been on the bullying side. All that remained of those hospital days was the bed, which had come with her, on loan from St Mark's. This continued its function of turning its occupant with the regularity imposed on it by the nursing sisters from London, who also saw to all Julie's physical needs. What with their constant ministrations, the turning from side to side, from front to back, day-long, night-long, Rosie's devotion, the visits of Dr Buckland and Miss Makepeace, and the hairdresser, Miriam, who called morning and afternoon to see to her hair and make-up, the days swung past, and Julie herself slipped into some sort of waking trance. Every minute was occupied, yet nothing happened. Nothing at all. Meals arrived punctually – preceded by Rosie, brandishing the menu and offering a glass of sherry. The day sister came on, went off for her meals –

when Rosie took over – finally departed, when the night sister appeared. A relief sister came with equal punctuality, while first the day and then the night sister took time off.

Each evening Rupert came in. Based now at the Halchester office of his firm, he told her about his day – the alterations to the West Wing, the interminable roof repairs, the plans for the cottages down by the Hard, the shrubs and trees to be planted by the new garage block, to screen the car parks from the house. He drank a glass of sherry with her – poured by Rosie, who enjoyed the small ritual – and after about an hour left for the main block to have dinner with Veronica and any guests she happened to be entertaining.

Julie had her dinner with Rosie. Afterwards the night sister began the long-drawn-out routine that eventually found Julie ready for drug-induced sleep – Dr Buckland's sleeping tablets seemed considerably more effective than those handed out at St Mark's, Julie found, and as a result the nights were a complete and welcome blank, free from pain or longing.

For longing, unfortunately, remained. Toby was still the centre of her existence, try as she might to push him out of her thoughts. This made her feel abominably guilty. She put herself out to be especially nice to Rupert each evening. She ought, she knew, to appreciate his constancy. According to the nursing sisters it was unusual. 'I must say, I do think you're lucky, Miss Alnaker, to have your fiancé coming in like this. So handsome, too, isn't he?' the older sister commented unfailingly each night.

Julie had to agree he was handsome, remembered how once his dark good looks had provided an answer to all her problems. How could it now be Toby's dishevelled angularity that lived beside her, produced this uproar in body and mind?

Toby had no place in her adult life. Admittedly as children they had planned to marry, had continued to take the idea seriously when Toby first went to medical school. But then it had seemed to die a natural death. Their horizons widened, their paths diverged, and to be honest, Julie was certain she herself had nourished the plan long after Toby had forgotten it. Just as she was nourishing it now. It was simply a childish dream, best forgotten.

Unfortunately, though, there was nothing childish about the feeling she had for Toby these days. He was a fever in her blood. Overpowering. Unwelcome. Devouring. Somehow he had managed to take possession. All she wanted was to be rid of him, forget him, turn safely back to Rupert. But Toby refused to leave, and the real-life Rupert remained obstinately flat and meaningless.

The real-life Toby had gone, though. No doubt of that. Back to the Central, back to the London life he knew. She had meant nothing to him, that was clear. He had been kind and gentle, like a considerate elder brother, looking after her while she was ill and in pain. But without even bothering to come in and say good-bye, he had returned to his hospital in London. Sending no message, even.

Now her only regular visitors were Rupert and Veronica, with Max at the weekends sometimes. She had no suspicion how many others would have looked in – Jo Grant, for instance, or Samantha, both of whom made several attempts, only to be put off each time by Rosie. Miriam too would have liked to pop in often, with gossip and chat – she and Julie had had an easy-going friendship for years. But Miriam, after all, was a very common girl, and Rosie had never thought this friendship quite the thing, so Miriam too was discouraged.

One Saturday morning, though, when Adam Trowbridge came in with Dr Buckland, he began talking about the plaster coming off, more X-rays, mobilizing Julie. She might begin sitting up in a wheelchair, doing more active exercises each day.

As a preliminary she found herself back in St Mark's – in a private room, though, this time. The tests were exhausting, while without the plaster she felt like a lobster ejected from its shell, vulnerable to any touch, each chance current of chilly air. As weak as a new kitten, and aching unceasingly.

Worst of all, though, was looking for Toby, expecting to see him round each corner. She knew perfectly well he was in London, of course. But her body hadn't, obviously, received the message. Her body continued to believe that as this was St Mark's, naturally Toby would be along any minute.

Finally, when the tests and the X-raying were ended, the consultations, proddings and conferences, they sent her home to Alnaker Hall, lying down still, but with a wheelchair in the ambulance, and instructions to sit up a little longer each day.

In practice, though, it proved not to be nearly as easy as they had made it sound. At first she was unable to sit up for more than five or ten minutes at a stretch, felt thoroughly ill throughout. Then, too, her body ached until she longed to scream, while her limbs were useless. For the first time she began to understand the length of the road she had to travel, and how much of her bodily fitness, previously taken so much for granted, had vanished, perhaps for ever.

The nursing sisters and the physiotherapist were bracing. So bracing, so demanding, that she began to hate them. Rosie, on the other hand, was protective, solicitous, gentle. 'Don't worry, Julie. It'll be all right in the end, there's no hurry. Take it easy, lie back until you feel more up to it. No one's going to make you do anything that upsets you, my pet. Not while I'm here.'

Dr Buckland came in, took one look at his patient, pale, subdued, a slip of a girl with tumbled hair, whom he'd known since babyhood. 'Take it easy, old dear,' he told her comfortingly. 'No hurry. You take it at your own pace.'

So Julie took it at her own pace. Or, to be strictly accurate, at Rosie's pace. The day sister, young and go-ahead, became frustrated and bored, talked of leaving for what she described as a more challenging post. In due course she went, and the night sister soon afterwards. A retired district nurse from Alnaker St Nicholas came in every evening to prepare Julie for bed, and Miss Makepeace continued to give her exercises and massage each morning.

The days began to form their own quiet and tranquil pattern. Punctually at eight thirty, tea was brought in by Rosie herself, who thoroughly enjoyed making it in the charming kitchen designed for the daughter of the house. The morning sun streamed in from across the park, sparked light off stainless steel and ceramic tiles, produced a warm glow from stripped pine. Rosie could hardly bear to think of the day when Julie would no longer need her, and she would once more be relegated to her flat in the staff quarters. So, willing time to stand still for ever, she measured out tea into the Georgian silver pot with meticulous care, lovingly assembled the Minton china, egg-shell thin, took it all in to Julie on the silver tray.

The tea was hot and invigorating. Both of them enjoyed it. After drinking a cup herself, and handing over the morning paper, Rosie would depart to the kitchen again to prepare their breakfast. Domestic bliss.

'Just coffee and toast,' Julie would say languidly. The effect of Dr Buckland's sleeping tablets was apt to linger and until she had drunk the coffee, a strong and pungent brew, she remained almost in a coma. After this, though, there would normally be a somewhat muddled rush – Rosie had never been able to keep track of time – before Miss Makepeace arrived, to begin her hour of physiotherapy.

The exercises were a form of torture, and after them Julie was always worn out, drank the glass of Lucozade prescribed by Dr Buckland and dozed off until it was time to face the next hurdle. Dressing. Not only difficult but exhausting. She usually managed to be ready in her wheelchair, though, when Miriam appeared to do her hair. Afterwards Rosie would push her into the lift and down into her sitting room, where she poured sherry with ceremonial precision from the heavy cut-glass decanter. Julie would select lunch from the menu typed out daily for her, and Rosie would ring down to the kitchens with her choice. Julie could, of course, quite well have dealt with this bit of telephoning herself, indeed it would have simplified matters considerably if she had done so, as Rosie tended to contradict herself in a flurry of flustered alterations guaranteed to exasperate the kitchen. They certainly exasperated Julie. But on the only occasion that she had taken the duty firmly into her own hands had done the ordering herself, Rosie had been so put out that she had never cared to repeat the experience. No need, she decided, to upset poor old Rosie.

They shared lunch at the little round table in the window, a slow and stately meal, taken at Rosie's speed. Slower and far more stately, in fact, than the quick snack Veronica and Samantha consumed together in the small family dining room next to the kitchens. The food, too, was not so hot. It had come a long way. Afterwards Rosie brewed coffee again, and then, as she put it, 'time for you to take the air, Julie'. Downstairs in the lift, then if it was fine Rosie would wheel her out to the terrace overlooking the rose garden, one of the few spots at the Hall traditionally reserved for the family, where, as Rosie assured her encouragingly, 'you can be quite undisturbed, dear. No one will bother you here.' Everywhere else in the gardens, of course, was not only open to the public between two and five in the afternoon on weekdays in summer, but busy with staff almost round the clock. There was a constant parade of architects, surveyors, engineers, interior decorators, painters, electricians, window cleaners. Then, of course, in addition to the students from the nearby horticultural college who saw to the gardens, there were the builders in the West Wing and the security staff on their patrols – these having been augmented recently. 'A lot of picture thefts lately,' Max explained. 'So Jo thought we should have more men on duty, and increase the frequency of the patrols. He wants them to have two-way radios, too, monitored by the switchboard. He's worked it all out – in fact, he's having himself a ball. Young Toby's gone back to London, apparently,' he added, darting a swift assessing glance.

'Yes,' Julie agreed briefly.

'Doing well, by all accounts,' Max commented, gave her a second penetrating look. Julie avoided it, and luckily Rosie came fussing along at that moment, and no more was said.

On days when the weather was chilly, Julie spent the afternoon in the orangery, and in any case tea was always brought to her here. Afterwards Rosie would push her back along the corridors to the Gatehouse, into the lift and up to her bedroom. She would have a wash, and Miriam would come in and comb out her hair, do her make-up for her, too, Rosie would push her back into the sitting room, and shortly afterwards Rupert would appear. He would ask how she was, and Rosie would pour them both a sherry, while Rupert told Julie about his own day. There was, unfortunately, little new to tell him about hers. Simply a history of aches and pains, and the same old routine.

Rupert was the first to disrupt this peaceful existence. As evening succeeded evening, and he made his way dutifully to the Gatehouse to sit with her, he found his visits increasingly onerous. The hour with Julie had long ago ceased to be a pleasure, had become a ritual he came to dread. His real enjoyment came afterwards, at Veronica's dinner table, where he was treated as the son of the house he had not yet become. This he valued, could not bring himself to relinquish, even while he daily looked for an escape from his appearances at the Gatehouse. Perhaps everything would have been all right, he thought with real anguish, if only they had been able to marry when they had planned. But this prolonged yet almost formal companionship was deathly – especially with Rosie popping in and out always like a jack-in-the-box and, he wouldn't be surprised to discover, listening at the door half the time. Even so, he had to admit, Rosie had her uses. For Rupert panicked badly at the prospect of taking over responsibility for Julie's care himself. She might be an invalid for years, Rupert knew, and at night his sleep began to be disturbed by dreams filled with anxiety. He was trying to manoeuvre a frail Julie in her wheelchair into situations where only one could pass. The excitement and anticipation he had once felt about his wedding had long ago vanished, leaving no trace, only increasing worry and pessimism.

He wasn't even happy in his mind about Veronica, either. Against his will, against every intention, she dominated him. He knew this and resented it, yet he was quite powerless to stop it. Every evening he was possessed by the same urge to please her, to do whatever she wanted, to win her approval. He despised himself for this, argued with himself about it, began almost to hate her simply because she could so easily exercise this rule over him. Love and hate fought within him, hopelessly mixed up with fear and trepidation. His approaching marriage had become an ordeal he dreaded yet had no wish to escape.

A complicated and unhappy situation, of which Veronica was quite unaware. She saw only a dutiful son-in-law, admiring and devoted, who would escort her as charmingly as she had once hoped her son James would. But James never wrote, even, and though she continued to miss him, always would, she was realistic too, and found Rupert an excellent substitute. She was delighted to think that Julie was bringing him permanently into the family. 'This is Rupert, who is to be my son-in-law, you know,' she introduced him everywhere, radiant with approval.

In an agonized attempt to restore Julie to her former place in his imagination, Rupert begged her to play her guitar again for him. Surely, he promised himself, when he saw her again bent over the instrument, beautiful and gentle, her long fingers plucking chords that would evoke so much past happiness, surely then he would love her as much as he had done in the past?

The idea startled Julie. 'My guitar? But–'

'You could play it sitting in your chair, couldn't you?'

'I suppose I could. But–'

'I'd love it if you did.'

'I'm so completely out of practice. I don't know if I–'

'You could try, couldn't you?' he pressed her desperately.

Touched by his intensity, guilty because of her own indifference, the next morning Julie asked Rosie to fetch the guitar, began to strum with fingers that turned out to be as clumsy and useless as the rest of her body.

'Don't wear yourself out,' Rosie adjured her, hovering, anxious, jealous of both Rupert and the guitar.

'I'm not,' Julie retorted sharply, irritated by her own incompetence as much as by Rosie's fussing. Her clumsy hands maddened her. Certainly she had told Rupert she would be out of practice, but she had expected to be a good deal better than this. Was there now no part of her body capable of responding to her wishes? Angry, frustrated, she sat raging in the orangery that afternoon. She didn't of course recognize it for a moment, but she had already crossed a Rubicon, become a typical convalescent, cross and snappy and ready for action.

Her hands, plucked angrily, discordantly, at the guitar, her mind circled elsewhere. Why, she asked herself bitterly, was she no longer in love with Rupert? Why was she so bored with him? Throughout her illness he had been loyal, faithful, kind, all any girl had a right to ask. Once he had swept her off her feet, and all she had wanted was to be his wife. What had become of their love? It had been genuine enough at the time, surely? Why did she have to long now for Toby, of all people, whom she'd known all her life, taken for granted for twenty years?

Perhaps that had been the trouble. Taking him for granted. Had she somehow assumed that, whoever else played a part in her life, Toby would remain there always? It had not been until she had suddenly found herself on a hospital bed, Toby and Rupert standing over her, sitting by her, appearing and disappearing, clearly – she had been forced to recognize – disliking one another, that she had understood that she might ever have to choose between them. At once, then, the answer came. Loud and clear. Inescapable.

If to have Rupert in her life meant losing Toby, then it was Rupert who must go.

A fine time she had chosen to make that discovery.

No more than an immature child, she saw now, silly and excitable, she had honestly believed she wanted to marry Rupert. But what she had really been after, had tried so hard to retain, had been no more than the unaccustomed thrill of admiration, of bring for once the centre of attention. The centre, too, of Rupert's world. She had never been this to anyone before. And then it had been a chance to make them all accept the fact that she was grown up, an adult with her own life to lead, her own marriage to arrange. She had even, she suspected, as she looked back into the past with eyes newly freed from illusion, been influenced by all the new clothes and the dressing up. Just as Toby had told her, in fact. But the end-product of this posturing had been marriage. Marriage to Rupert until the end of her days, until she was old, with children and grandchildren. For ever.

But it was Toby she wanted for ever, she knew that now. Rupert had been no more than a brief infatuation.

She could never tell him this, though.

And Toby had forgotten her.

Strumming on the guitar with fingers already tender and painful from the lack of practice, she made ugly crashing discords, hateful sounds for a hateful world.

Rosie she had sent off to hunt out her music, longing only to be alone for once, alone to brood. Over how love had died. And how love lived on.

And she raised her eyes from her guitar and saw Toby, striding towards her across the rose garden, through the crimson blooms and the white, the yellow and scarlet. An answer to prayer, a response to her desperate anguish.

Everything was going to be all right, after all. She smiled brilliantly, joyfully, let her guitar drop, held out her hands in welcome.

CHAPTER FIVE

Toby

Everything turned out to be far from right. Toby at once put a prompt end to the vague imaginings Julie had been indulging.

'Good grief,' he greeted her unflatteringly. 'What a fearful little podge.'

Julie knew, of course, that she had been putting on weight. But it was another matter to have it pointed out in this harsh and unsympathetic fashion. Her loving thoughts shattered, she was ready to hit Toby. Hard.

But worse was to come.

'Spotty, too,' he added, as he came nearer and peered at her with the worst sort of brotherly attention. 'The sooner you go on a diet the better.'

At that moment, Julie's sore fingers would very much have enjoyed throttling Toby. She regarded him with hatred, coupled with a distinct sense of injustice. He had brutally let her down. Could this be the hero of whom she had been dreaming throughout long months? This tousled, inconsiderate oaf?

'Oaf,' she said clearly, determined to punish him for having let her down like this. 'Exactly as mother has always said, you're nothing but an oaf.' Immediately she wished the words unsaid. Somewhere inside her a voice screamed denial.

Toby, naturally enough, knew nothing of this, looked her over with a dislike the equal of her own, retorted in kind. 'Spoilt baby,' he said. 'Spoilt, rude, fat baby. In a push chair, too,' he added the final insult.

This was outrageous. He was supposed, after all, to be a doctor. Surely at least he understood... Julie, not at all unlike an angry baby, grew red in her undeniably fat face, appeared to be about to explode.

Toby surveyed the phenomenon calmly. He'd planned to enrage her. Obviously he'd succeeded. Adam had told him a week or two earlier that Julie had come to a full stop in her progress towards recovery. She was simply sitting about, doing nothing, needed jerking out of her apathy before it was too late, he said, mentioning too that she had put on far too much weight.

'I've advised all of them, Julie herself, her mother, and Dr Buckland, that she ought to go to a Rehabilitation Centre at this stage.

Get fully mobilized. But Buckland argues it's too soon, and I can't do more than advise, of course. So between him and the patient – eating three square meals a day and doing very little else, as far as I can make out – there's damn all happening. If you're going down for your weekend off, you might see how the land lies, try to galvanize your girl friend in to activity.'

'She's not my girl friend,' Toby had said, more shortly than was customary when speaking to his former chief.

But he had gone down to the Hall, talked first to his father, then gone over to see Dr Buckland. 'How do you think Julie is?' he'd asked him. 'By all accounts she seems to have settled into some sort of comfortable rut with old Rosie dancing attendance. Don't you think it's more than time she got moving?'

'You may call it a rut, my boy,' Dr Buckland had said placidly. Toby had been querying his methods since he'd first had the run of the surgery at the age of ten or so. 'What's this for? Why do you use it? Wouldn't it be better if you...?' Dr Buckland had never taken much notice, and he didn't propose to start worrying now. 'You must remember that Julie suffered major injuries, Toby. No reason why she shouldn't have the benefit of a slow and steady convalescence, that I can see. After all, her family can afford to have her properly cared for, there's no job she has to get back to, no household she has to run. Once she is fit, too, there'll be all the stress of a big wedding to be gone through. Why rush matters?'

'I know all about the wedding,' Toby said curtly.

'The trouble with all you young men,' Dr Buckland went on, ignoring the interjection – 'among other things, of course' – he twinkled affably, 'is that you aren't content to stand back, quietly watching events. You have to be everlastingly interfering. A mistake, in my opinion. Granted it may make the doctor feel powerful, it's not necessarily at all good for the patient. Eh? What? You don't agree? You will one day. Let nature take its course,' he advised soothingly, began to fill his pipe. 'Unwise to interrupt the natural process of convalescence.' Newly qualified young men from teaching hospitals, he added, getting well into his stride, were only too apt to assume they knew all the answers, treat their patients like so many mathematical equations.

Toby did not, as it happened, feel he was

in any danger of treating Julie as a mathematical equation.

Medicine, indeed, was becoming too scientific by far. 'You could all do with a spell in general practice. Surgery on the kitchen table,' Dr Buckland announced, retreating a couple of generations further into the past, 'would have taught you a thing or two.'

Silly old buffer, Toby thought irreverently. But he battled respectfully but inexorably on, eventually extorting the unwilling admission that at this stage it might certainly do no actual harm for Julie to go to some sort of rehabilitation centre, provided she herself felt ready for it. 'Not otherwise,' he said firmly. 'I won't have the poor girl forced into any line of treatment she is at all unhappy about.'

'Of course not,' Toby agreed heartily, pleased to have brought him this far. The rest would be up to Julie. He set off across the park at the brisk jog-trot that since he qualified had become his most usual method of progress.

Now all he had to do was jolt Julie into action. And he knew exactly how to achieve that, of course. Put her into a tearing rage. After that, there would be no holding her.

Stage one satisfactorily attained, he observed.

Scarlet-faced, furious, she bellowed at him. 'Is it my fault I'm in this thing?' She hit the sides of the wheelchair.

At this moment, Toby spotted the guitar, abandoned on the ground.

'Sitting about and strumming madrigals,' he snorted. 'When you ought to be on your two feet.'

This was beyond everything. He had not even troubled to find out the facts. 'You haven't even bothered to find out how I am,' she accused him, her voice, to her extreme annoyance trembling on the edge of tears. 'I *can't* walk, however much I want to.'

'Never know until you try,' he said cheerfully. 'Trouble is, you haven't got as far as trying, have you?'

She was indignant. 'You don't know what it's like–'

'I can see what it's like. You must have put on nearly forty pounds. How do you expect to learn to walk again, humping all that extra weight about?'

Oddly enough, it had never occurred to Julie that her increased weight would have any effect on her ability to mobilize her slack and useless legs. She stared uncertainly at Toby.

'You ought to go on a strict diet. At once.

95

Lose at least twenty pounds first of all, then go in daily to the Rehabilitation Centre at St Mark's. You'll lose the next twenty pounds easily once you're there each day, be on your feet in a couple of months.'

Was it possible?

'Don't you realize you're wasting valuable time, lolling about in that damned chair all day?'

'I'm not lolling. I'm trying to play my guitar. You may think that's lolling, but I can assure you it isn't. It's abominably difficult. I've got sore fingers, for one thing.' She spread them before him.

This got her nowhere.

'And a sore bottom too, I shouldn't wonder,' Toby rejoined, with unwelcome accuracy. An unfriendly pause ensued.

'Well, what am I supposed to do, according to you?' Julie demanded, breaking the arctic silence that had descended.

'I've told you. Go to the Rehabilitation Centre. Exercise until you drop. Apart from that, you need a better chair than that. Battery-powered, so that you can move around independently.'

'Battery-powered?' Dr Buckland had never mentioned this possibility.

'Ring up the hospital and ask. They'll tell

you how to get hold of one. Personally, I don't see why you shouldn't drive yourself around in a car, as well. No need to be chained to poor old Rosie and this place.' If she was able to move around under her own steam, he thought, she'd have other interests than food, find it easier to diet. She could confine her guitar-playing to the evenings, too. Entertain that smug Rupert with it then, no doubt. Everyone at the Hall was aware that Rupert had proposed to Julie after he had seen her playing her guitar at the *Son et Lumière,* and the truth was that the mere sight of the instrument made Toby sick with jealousy.

'Drive myself?' she was asking. 'How can I?'

Toby pulled himself together. He'd planned his strategy with care, must not allow himself to wander off into unhappy emotional byways and forget what he was here for. Nothing to do with him what Rupert and Julie did in their future together. First things first. Julie must be mobilized for her own good. If it also happened to be for Rupert's good, that, Toby reminded himself, was nothing to do with him.

'Easily,' he said crisply. 'All you have to do is ask Dad to arrange for one of the cars to be converted to manual controls.'

She looked at him dubiously. Entirely unmechanical, she had had no idea that anything like this would be possible.

'If you have any desire to be independent, that is,' Toby added.

The force of his pain hit her. Knowing nothing of what caused it, she assumed he was condemning her for what he evidently regarded as feebleness.

His next inquiry reinforced his view. 'Or are you proposing to remain a passenger for the rest of your days?' he demanded sarcastically.

'Dr Buckland said—'

'Rest and fresh air and good food, I've no doubt. All very well in their place. But those days should be behind you. It's more than time you got cracking. If you don't want to take my word for it, ask Adam Trowbridge. And anyway, lose some of that extra weight. You look like an obese toddler. And for God's sake get yourself out of this cosy little backwater. Not at the age of retirement yet, are you?'

Julie flushed.

'Of course, you'll find it hard going. Nothing like as easy as sitting there and strumming away on your guitar. Your body won't like it at all at first, you'll very likely be in pain most of the time. It's a damn difficult thing you have to do, you'll be tired out every day. Exhausted, if you do as much as you should. But you'll never learn to walk again and lead a normal life by sitting about here in a chair and fattening yourself up like a Christmas goose.'

At this inopportune moment, to Julie's acute embarrassment, a vast silver tea-tray arrived, complete with sandwiches, fruit cake, cream cakes and chocolate biscuits. It was closely followed by Rosie, bearing a great sheaf of music. Toby, not surprisingly, regarded both with a sardonic and distinctly cold eye, his bony features adopting what Rosie afterwards informed Veronica was an expression of callous contempt. 'He came storming in and thoroughly upset Julie this afternoon,' she said. 'If only I'd been there, I would soon have put a stop to it. Julie's been in a state ever since. And he's supposed to be a doctor, too. What it must be like to be a patient of his in the wards at that hospital I shudder to think.' She shuddered appropriately, if somewhat theatrically.

'Opinionated young upstart,' Veronica commented irritably, conveniently overlooking the fact that she could equally well have been described in exactly these terms herself – and, indeed, by the more diehard members of the aristocracy often had been.

The upstart, on his way back to the Central, carried with him an unnerving picture of a fat, chubby Julie, flushed and almost certainly on the brink of tears. Surprisingly, he felt far closer to her when she looked like this than he had done when she appeared so fashionable and poised. Today she had reminded him strongly of herself when much younger, and what he longed to do was to take her into his arms and comfort her.

His emotions in turmoil once more, he began to wish he hadn't set eyes on her, only to cancel the thought immediately. He had needed to see her. Adam, as usual, had been right. She was sinking into an indolent apathy, could easily throw her entire future away, drift into permanent invalidism, cherished and looked after for ever, no life of her own. She had to be shocked out of this attitude before it was too late. Before she grew too fat, and limbs, so long unused, lost all strength and power.

Well, he reckoned he'd shocked her all right. But he could take no pride in his achievement. Had he honestly had to go out of his way to antagonize her? What sort of doctor was he if he could find no other method of mobilizing an invalid, a sick girl in a wheelchair, than by abusing her like a market porter? He was ashamed of himself.

Back in the Central on Sunday night, he did a stony, tight-lipped round at midnight, for good measure quarrelled with the staff nurse he'd recently been taking out.

At the Hall they found Julie in an appalling mood. This was made considerably worse by Rosie's well-meaning sympathy, though Julie found it difficult to understand why this staunch support should seem so tiresome.

'If you ask me,' Rosie sniffed fiercely,. 'Toby Grant is little more than a young hooligan.'

'I called him an oaf,' Julie remembered.

'Exactly what he is,' Rosie approved.

'What he said was right.' Julie glared, her eyes unusually bright. 'Absolutely right. I am far too fat.'

'Dr Buckland said we should build you up.'

'What needs building is muscle, not fat,' Julie responded dogmatically.

Rosie recognized the signs only too well. Julie had begun to speak with Toby's voice. As she had often pointed out to Veronica in the past, he had always had far too much influence over Julie.

'Now have your lunch, and stop worrying about anything that wretched boy may have said. Dr Buckland is looking after you, not Master Toby Grant.'

'I don't want any potatoes,' Julie said.

As soon as Miss Makepeace arrived, she began cross-examining her about the Rehabilitation Centre in Halchester.

'Oh, I don't think that would be at all suitable for you, Miss Alnaker.'

'Why not?'

'Well, of course they do very good work there, but I don't think you'd care for it. Now the other leg, shall we? *Good.* That's the way. *Push.* And again. Now, I want to feel you pushing against my hand. That's it. And *up* we go.'

'Why wouldn't I care for it?' Julie persevered, raising and lowering her legs in turn, the motive-power supplied by Miss Makepeace.

'Well, honestly, Miss Alnaker, the people you'd meet there wouldn't be quite your sort of person, you know. *Again.* Goo – ood.'

'What sort of person–'

'What I mean is, Miss Alnaker, you see – well, you've led rather a sheltered life here, haven't you? And–'

'I haven't. I–'

'Oh, but you have really, Miss Alnaker, though you may not realize it. But I'm afraid you'd find it a wee bit of a change if you went to the Centre. It wouldn't be at all the thing. Now the arms, shall we? Left arm *bend*. Good. And again.'

Lips compressed, Julie did arms bend, said no more. But the following afternoon when Dr Buckland paid one of his visits, recently more of a social occasion than a clinical examination, she tackled him.

'The Rehabilitation Centre?' he echoed, equally horrified. 'My dear Julie, no. Not at all the type of place for you. The National Health service ... all very fine in its way, of course ... some excellent results at the Centre, too, I'm bound to admit. But I wouldn't think of referring one of my private patients there. Er – perhaps finding Miss Makepeace a little trying, my dear? I know she can be somewhat wearing. And day after day, no wonder if–'

'No, it's not Miss Makepeace,' Julie said hastily, seeing the physiotherapist about to be withdrawn. 'It's just that I don't seem to be making any progress, so I thought if I–'

'You must try to retain an optimistic outlook, my dear. And be patient. Every long-term disability demands this, I am afraid. I can understand the days must drag. But you have the television, haven't you? A great boon for people at home all day. And perhaps some needlework wouldn't come amiss, do you think? Embroidery, say? My mother in her later years found her tapestry work engrossing, I remember.'

Julie simmered inwardly.

Not, though, as inwardly as she had imagined. Dr Buckland was not slow, picked up her reaction at once. 'Don't care for the idea? No. A little out of date, I expect. I'm becoming old-fashioned, I fear.' He thought momentarily, brightened. 'How about learning a language, then? I believe you can do it from recordings these days.' He beamed benevolently. 'Or should I say *discs?*'

'Probably.' Julie was abrupt, gruff.

Amazing how like her father the child could be, Dr Buckland mused. And thinking of Lord Alnaker, he had another idea. 'Chess, now?' he suggested. 'How about that? An absorbing interest.'

'Who would I play with?' Julie pulled a face. 'Not Rosie.'

'No, I fear not. Quite so. M – mm – ah. Indeed, that would undoubtedly be the difficulty, except when your father is down. Of

104

course, there's always the bishop.' He hesitated doubtfully.

Julie had had enough of this. 'Do you think I'm too fat?' she demanded.

'Too fat?' He did think so, had been wondering how to work round to it. 'Well, my dear, I must admit, not as slim as you used to be, eh?' He patted her cheek. 'Speaking for myself, of course, nothing I like better than to see a nice rounded cheek with a charming dimple. But I think we must say that you could with advantage keep a rather stricter eye on your diet. Cut down a little on starch, perhaps? Let me see, exactly what is your weight now, mm – ah? Yes, ye – es. Indeed. I think only one slice of toast at breakfast, don't you? No roll and butter at lunch or dinner? If you could manage to cut out potatoes, too, that would be an excellent plan, you know. And not too many little cakes at tea time, eh?'

'You couldn't give me a diet to follow, or something like that?'

'Oh, no need to go to quite those lengths. Simply exercise a little discretion, cut down on bread and cakes, not too many sweets and chocolates. I think you'll find it'll answer.'

'And you really don't think I should go to

the Centre in Halchester?'

'Hardly. You'd find yourself a fish out of water, I'm afraid. No, no, you wouldn't care for it at all.'

On her mettle now, made more obstinate by the opposition she had met, Julie was becoming determined to follow Toby's suggestions, go at all costs to this Centre. She'd show them. Sheltered, was she?

On Saturday morning, when Adam Trowbridge arrived she raised the question again. Dr Buckland displayed alarm, while Adam concealed a grin.

'Not a bad idea,' he said cheerfully. 'But you'll need to lose some weight first, young woman. Far too plump. How are you proposing to heave all that surplus fat around, eh? I warn you, you'll find sweating it off hard going, won't she, Buckland? Better go on a fairly stiff diet for a month first, get the physio to step up your exercises at the same time. Then try the Centre at St Mark's when you've lost some of that extra weight.'

Dr Buckland didn't care for the look of things, but he couldn't quite see how to proceed. His problem was that he remembered perfectly well that when Adam Trowbridge had been Director of the Accident Unit at St Mark's himself, he had also been

106

in charge of the Rehabilitation Centre, and he didn't quite see how to inform him it wasn't good enough for the Hon. Julia Alnaker. So he coughed, wondered if perhaps Miss Makepeace couldn't manage very nicely, you know, with the extra exercises – an excellent notion, that, yet, indeed – and then there was the diet too, that might be, might it not, enough to be going on with, wouldn't you say?

Adam agreed amiably that it would be a month at least before Julie was ready for the Centre. He thought, though, they'd be well advised to book her in immediately. There was always a waiting list. 'I'll get my secretary to lay it on,' he promised, and said good-bye to Julie.

Going down in the lift with Dr Buckland he remarked casually, 'By the way, we've quite a good thousand-calorie-diet sheet we find very useful these days. I'll tell my secretary to send one to the Alnakers, shall I?' He nodded agreeably, walked briskly out to his Volvo. 'We'll meet again next week, then,' he added, already at the wheel, raised a hand in salute, and drove off. Dr Buckland was left in the drive asking himself exactly what had happened? How had he come to allow himself to be outmanoeuvred, almost before he could turn round?

On Monday morning, Adam ran across Toby, who was working now as a house physician on the professional medical unit, and congratulated him on a crafty bit of patient management.

Toby's long bony face, lately inclined to gloom, Adam had noticed, at once lighted up. 'Did it come off, then, sir? You mean Julie's going to the Rehabilitation Centre?'

'Not only that, I've sent her a thousand-calorie-diet sheet.' Adam grinned broadly.

Toby began to emit a triumphant crow, hastily recollected himself, swallowed it and said, 'I thought my talk might pay off. How did Dr Buckland take it? Is he going to be–' He swallowed another sound, gulped. He'd been about to say 'is he going to be obstructive?' But it wouldn't do. Adam would never stand for this type of comment on a respected elderly colleague.

'I don't think he's too happy about our achievements you know,' Adam said. 'But Julie seems hell bent on losing weight and going to the Centre, so I've booked her in a month from now. It's simply a question of whether she can keep the pace up. She's going to need a great deal of stamina and endurance if she's to attain full mobility.

Has she got it, would you say? She looks such a child sometimes, I must say I can understand why old Buckland feels the Centre will be too much for her. He may prove to be right, you realize.'

'It won't be too much once she gets there.' Toby was sure of this. 'Julie has loads of grit and determination. She can always hang on when things are difficult. What she can't do is get started. Especially not against opposition from inside her family. She usually assumes they must be right and she must be wrong, you see. And normally it's the other way round.'

'Miss Penrose isn't exactly a help, either. Or so it strikes me. Wants to wrap the girl in cotton wool.'

'Always been like that,' Toby commented briefly.

'You evidently have the entire set-up taped,' Adam said. 'I'll apply to you if I run into any problems.'

Toby frowned. 'It's only that we grew up together,' he explained. Then he astonished himself by coming out with the shame that had been eating away at him. 'And even then I couldn't pull it off without having a row with the girl, thoroughly upsetting her. I can't say I come out of it very well.'

'Oh, my dear lad,' Adam exclaimed. 'I know so well how you feel. That's always been my problem. I agree with you absolutely, one does feel there ought to be some method of mobilizing the sick and injured, other than having a stand-up fight, no holds barred. And though it remains some consolation to see them active and enjoying life as a result of one's efforts, I do rather suspect, you know, that not everyone finds it essential to quarrel with them merely in order to ginger them up.'

'Julie may not forgive me,' Toby said morosely. This conviction had accompanied him for days.

'But at least she has a good chance of being unforgiving on her two feet, instead of friendly in a wheelchair. That's the thought you have to hang on to.'

'I suppose so,' Toby agreed, but with no appreciable lightening of the misery that had overtaken him.

'And in the meantime you can try brushing up on your tact and bedside manner,' Adam ended. He smiled cheerfully and encouragingly, but his eyes were gentle. He felt extraordinarily sorry for this former house surgeon of his. He'd had one hard knock, Adam was sure of it, when this girl Julie

Alnaker decided to marry her architect. And now, if that was not enough to be going on with, he was almost certainly due to receive a second blow. His future had been hanging in the balance for months, but, if the grapevine was to be believed, the edict had gone out. Inside a week Toby Grant would learn that he had no chance of a career as a physician at the Central. It would be the end of his hopes. The end of his contract, too.

CHAPTER SIX

The Central London Hospital

Orthopaedic surgery, as Adam had known from the beginning, had never been Toby Grant's first choice. It had been the hospital's choice for him. From his student days he had been marked down as a potential surgeon, possibly even an outstanding one, provided he was capable of the necessary unremitting application – for this was a calling that demanded real dedication, twenty-four hours a day, seven days a week.

Of course, they had always known how to pick them at the Central, and from the start of his first year they had read Toby Grant loud and clear – and much more accurately than he had even been able to read himself. As Adam Trowbridge had commented to the dean of the medical school when the question of Toby's first pre-registration post had come up, 'Toby may like to think he's an intellectual, but in fact he's not an academic type at all. Oh, he can hit the books when he has to, I'll give him that, but for him it's simply a means to an end. He's not top brain, just a thoroughly practical lad. Sensible, reliable, good with his hands, well organized.'

'In short, a surgeon,' the dean had suggested, with a broad grin. 'And you want him. You take him, then.' He'd made a note on his list against Toby's name, and as a result he had been appointed as Adam's house surgeon. He'd done six months in this post, and it had been Adam who had arranged for him to go to St Mark's for the following six months. Toby had known he ought to consider himself lucky to have been recommended by Adam himself for the post there, with the prospect, too, if he continued to do well, of going back to the orthopaedic wards at the Central. Many envied him his chances.

And he had done well. Adam had been pleased with him, had found him another post. But not the post they had all forecast, on the orthopaedic unit. Not on the surgical side at all. For Toby had never been anything but honest – if not transparent – and Adam was well aware that this particular young surgeon was eating his heart out for a chance to prove himself on the medical side. He was fond of Toby by now, beginning to find him quite a useful assistant too, but he had no intention of having Toby permanently on his staff unless he was prepared to make orthopaedic surgery his career, and devote himself to it completely. So, with an eye to the future, it must be admitted – a future that Adam saw quite differently from Toby – Adam persuaded the pundits into trying young Grant on the medical unit.

He had completed five months of the six months appointment now, and Adam cornered the Professor of Medicine, Sir Ivor Carey, inquired about Toby. Exactly as gossip had warned Adam, Carey was noticeably unenthusiastic about his latest recruit. 'Of course, I've had far worse,' he began.

'Far better too, I suppose?'

'Frankly, yes. Once his appointment comes to an end, I must admit I shan't be sorry to see the back of him. Not that he isn't hard working. Reliable, too, in his way. But he's not really up to our standard, you know – not registrar material, for instance. Or not on this unit. May be elsewhere, of course. After all, this is still a teaching hospital, and…' He went on to explain in pedantic detail what in his opinion might be expected of registrars on professional medical units in teaching hospitals, made it abundantly clear that Toby wouldn't make the grade. 'I've told the dean so,' he ended. No further post for Toby Grant, that meant.

Adam went into action. 'Agreed that he's not going to set the Thames alight academically, in my opinion he had considerable promise as a surgeon. In the theatre he's quick and highly organized, you know. Deft, too, and gentle. Good results, we found.'

Carey raised his eyebrows, tapped his forehead. 'Not enough up here.'

Adam was irritated. Supercilious smug physicians, he thought, not for the first time. 'I could still do with him on the orthopaedic unit.'

'Then you have him, my boy,' the older man said. 'And welcome. He's a nice enough lad, I'll grant you that. Clinically his judgement is sound enough. Within limits, of course. But can you see him getting the membership first go, for instance?' He shrugged. 'Several bites at the cherry may do for them out in the provinces, but it's hardly good enough here at the Central, is it?'

Adam, who had spent years in the provinces himself, bit back an angry retort. Over the years he had learnt wisdom. Aloud he said, 'I fancy he'll make a useful orthopod. But I'm not having him unless he's

115

willing to apply himself wholeheartedly. I don't want him if he imagines he's simply filling a gap, waiting around until he succeeds in landing another medical post. So if I fit him in, will you break it to the unfortunate soul that he has positively no future on the medical side?'

'No trouble there. I have difficulty in not making it plain to him daily,' Carey rejoined. 'But I daresay you'll be able to train him up into an excellent craftsman,' he added kindly, went on his way. Adam fumed. Craftsman, indeed. To Sir Ivor Carey, of course, all surgeons were 'mere craftsmen', unless they became, worst still, 'useful technicians' instead. Damned nerve, Adam thought. In his book, young Toby Grant was worth two of the eminent professor's namby-pamby young men.

He sighed. Life could be very unfair. You only had to take a look round the wards to see that. And now here was Toby, capable and hardworking, steadfast and loyal, too. But this was far from being enough for Sir Ivor Carey. The fact that Toby was much better suited to surgery would be no help to him at all when the blow struck.

In fact Adam was doing the Professor of Medicine an injustice. He could be kind and understanding when he chose, as many of his patients would have testified. It was a pity, of course, that the inclination to exercise these qualities seldom seized him. When he was not busily engaged in cutting his staff down to size, he could be comparatively human. The next day he took Toby on one side, discussed his future with him patiently and with a sensitivity that would have astonished Adam. He even went so far as to inform Toby that the surgeons were asking for him back, and he, Sir Ivor Carey, friend to all mankind, was in the circumstances prepared to make something of a sacrifice. Luckily for him, Toby didn't quite fall for this improbable story, and just as well, too. Immediately after it came the stab to the heart. 'After all, we both have to recognize, don't we, that you'll never make a senior medical registrar on this unit, let alone obtain a consultant post.' He paused momentarily, long enough for the words to sink in. 'I think we must take that for granted, wouldn't you agree?' Another infinitesimal pause, not long enough though, for agreement, which he did indeed take for granted. 'I'm afraid we must face that, you know. Don't think I haven't found you thoroughly useful. Yes indeed, a most useful *and* zealous member of our little team, heh? Don't for one moment assume I've failed to appreciate your undoubted capacity for hard work–'

Toby squirmed. Useful, zealous and hard-working. Virtue had never seemed so unattractive.

'–but that isn't quite enough for the medical unit here at the Central, is it, my boy?' A sudden, slightly unconvincing, try for the fatherly approach. 'So I think we must agree that you haven't a future on the medical side, mustn't we?'

Toby set his lips.

'But, as I say, the surgeons consider you may have one with them. If you take my advice, you'll get back where you belong, on the orthopaedic unit, where they appear to want you.' Surgeons apparently had odd tastes. 'It seems you might be able to expect a registrar's post there. Let me see now, when did you qualify?'

Toby told him.

'Ah yes. Well, early days, my boy, early days. But in my opinion you'd be well advised to think seriously about surgery from now on.' He nodded kindly. That was that. He looked at his watch. 'I think I can just fit Mrs Swithinbank in before I go. Now, tell

118

me, how did she respond to the changed steroid dosage?'

Toby pulled himself together, thought about Mrs Swithinbank and steroids. They both went to see her. Afterwards he trod dutifully down to the courtyard and saw his chief into his pearl-grey Daimler, returned to the wards to institute the various new drug regimes Carey had prescribed. Here he glared ferociously at the staff nurse with whom he'd quarrelled a week earlier. Newly back on days after her spell of night duty, she had been hoping to make it up with him, return to their previous easy friendship. Obviously, though, she saw, she remained unforgiven, a black mark against her for ever. Goodbye, Toby Grant. It was fun knowing you.

Toby, in fact, hadn't even seen her. Locked into his own misery, he was contemplating total failure. Unwanted, rejected – first by Julie, now by the medicine he'd set his heart on.

He moved stolidly round the ward, unconscious of the staff nurse with him. Alive, though, to the patients under his care. And slowly, to his amazement, he began feeling better. He wasn't, after all, useless. Here he was, bringing not only treatment but some

119

kind of comfort and reassurance to these fellow human beings in so much pain and distress. All right, he wasn't the Central's wonder boy, hadn't made the grade with the Professor of Medicine. But he made it with these patients. Every time. He had a part to play in this hospital, that he'd originally joined as a raw student.

He had learnt an enormous amount on the medical unit, he knew. He might not be the best they'd ever had, but he'd go back to the surgical side far better equipped to do his job as a result of this past six months. And it was something, too, even if Sir Ivor Carey didn't see it, to know that the orthopaedic unit wanted him. He might be no more than a pair of hands, but he had a contribution to make.

And what was more, he was finding his own place in this great teaching hospital that had trained him. He had a sense of belonging. His eye passed rapidly down the case notes he'd been writing up, he shuffled them back into order again, gave a broad smile to the astonished and relieved staff nurse, and left the ward fast in search of his registrar.

He'd jerked Julie into some sort of useful action, too, he remembered as he swung along the corridors. The part he played in her life was not the one he would have chosen, either. But it might be vital.

What he didn't know was that down at Alnaker Hall Rosie was doing her best to reduce the effect of his interference. Although she would never knowingly have sacrificed Julie's health or recovery to her own convenience, she had been counting on looking after her more or less for ever. Even after her marriage to Rupert, Rosie had expected to be there, seeing to everything that a semi-invalid could not be asked to manage for herself.

Suddenly, though, to her consternation, the invalid was preparing to take up her bed and walk. There might no longer be any place for Rosie at Alnaker Hall. Too late, she grasped the mistake she had made in ever having allowed Samantha to take over her secretarial duties. For if Julie was to spend all day at the Rehabilitation Centre what would there be left for Rosie to do? She could hear Veronica saying it, presenting her with her final salary cheque.

And Rosie loved the Hall almost more than the Alnakers. Her entire life had been spent in its shadow. She could hardly imagine an existence not bounded by its rose-pink Tudor walls, its leaded windows overlooking rose gardens and lawns, spreading cedars, well-clipped topiary and the Grecian statues that the seventh viscount had looted. Her father had been Vicar of Alnaker St Nicholas for fifty years, and Rosie had shared a governess with the Buckland girls, now all scattered, had grown up to run troops of guides and brownies, jumble sales, fetes and Christmas bazaars. She had more than welcomed the opportunity, in her early thirties, of becoming Julie's governess – her first paid employment. Julie had been only three then, and Rosie had taught her until she went to boarding school at twelve. In those days she had bicycled in daily from the vicarage, and as Veronica's secretary had continued to do so. Eventually, when her father had retired, Max Alnaker had given him one of the cottages down by the Hard, and the family had lived there until Canon Penrose had died, well into his eighties, and then Rosie's mother had followed him within a few months. Veronica had suggested then that Rosie should move into a flat in the staff wing, and she had been thankful to do so. But now, what was to become of her? These last few months she had been living in a fool's paradise, she realized. Somehow she had to safeguard her position.

She began with Veronica. 'Totally unsuit-able, it seems to me,' she said to her, 'to attempt to throw a gentle, sensitive girl like Julie into a place like the Rehabilitation Centre at Halchester. Miss Makepeace tells me it's really intended for factory workers and lorry drivers with broken limbs. People like that. I can't imagine what Mr Trow-bridge can possibly be thinking of. Rather a rough diamond himself, isn't he?' she ended hopefully.

'Certainly he struck me as distinctly un-couth,' Veronica agreed with a snap. 'But Max seems to consider him very *clever.*' She paused disparagingly. In Veronica's eyes, to be couth was much more essential than to be clever. 'I must say, now that Julie is having Miss Makepeace twice daily, I can't see what advantage is to be gained by travelling into Halchester instead to this wretched Centre. Obviously she won't get anything like the individual attention she's receiving now. Apart from the fact that, as you say, the place is bound to be overcrowded and rough. I didn't at all care for the atmosphere in St Mark's, either, and I daresay the Centre will be just as bad.' She shrugged. 'Well, I'll talk to Max about it. And Rupert too. Perhaps he'll be able to talk Julie out of this idiotic notion. In fact, I wonder, you know, if it might not be a good idea for them to have a little holiday together.' She pondered, her long and beautiful fingers toying with her slim ivory paper knife.

Veronica's office had once been the house-keeper's room, and, tucked away in the servants' wing, had escaped the face-lift administered to the main block in the eighteenth century. In this room the afternoon sun came slanting still through mullioned windows with the original leaded casements, tiny squares of old glass, struck auburn lights from her hair.

'Wouldn't you think,' she went on, having examined her latest plan and found it excellent, 'that it would do Julie good, after this dreary time the poor dear has been through ever since her accident, to go abroad to some real sun? The South of France, say, or Italy. Or perhaps Greece.'

Rosie goggled. As usual, Veronica had moved too fast for her.

'You would have to go with her, of course, and Miss Makepeace, to keep up her exercises and look after her.'

Rosie agreed ecstatically.

'Rupert could take you out, stay for a

while to see you settled in,' Veronica added confidently. That either Rupert or his senior partner might not consider his time entirely at her disposal failed to occur to her. And after all, since the Alnaker estate contract was the biggest – and easily the most influential – the firm had, she was probably correct in her assumption. 'I might even get away for a week or two myself for a brief rest,' she added, the prospect growing on her.

It grew on Rosie, too. However, she saw breakers ahead, felt compelled to sound a note of warning. 'I don't quite know how Julie will take it, Lady Alnaker. You know how obstinate she can be sometimes, and she does seem to have set her heart on going to this ridiculous Centre at St Mark's. Of course, she hasn't the slightest idea what it'll be like.'

'Rupert can talk to her,' Veronica promised.

And so, two evenings later, over the glass of dry sherry that he secretly detested, Rupert did his stuff.

'Julie darling,' he began cautiously, having been warned by Veronica that his assignment might not prove easy. 'You're looking dreadfully pale and tired. Between this slimming business and all these exercises, you're thoroughly worn out and run down.'

Julie stared at him. 'Thanks,' she said. 'Great.'

'No wonder,' Rupert said hastily, 'after all these months of illness. That's just the point. I'd like to get you away for a good holiday. I think you should have a complete change before you go to this Rehabilitation Centre. Your parents say we could go to the Adriatic coast. There's a villa there, over-looking the sea your father could borrow – fully staffed and so on.' It belonged, in fact, to one of Max's partners, who used it for only about six weeks in every year. 'Wonderful climate, superb scenery. We could fly out, you and I, and of course we'd have to take Rosie and Miss Makepeace too, so that you could keep up the good work, eh?' He looked at her hopefully. He'd never been to the Adriatic coast.

CHAPTER SEVEN

St Mark's, Halchester

Everyone was fed up to the teeth with Julie. There they were, all longing to go to the Adriatic. Only the invalid, for whose benefit the trip had been planned, refused to budge.

It seemed to Julie she was under constant attack. One by one they had a go at her, came to see her to point out how much good it would do her to travel to the sun, to have a change, to make a break, be more enterprising. Above all, to allow herself to be transported with them to the sun-drenched Adriatic coast.

'Not until I've finished with this wheelchair,' Julie reiterated, exactly as Rosie had foreseen. It was hard to be done out of the holiday of a lifetime, simply because Julie couldn't, or wouldn't, see what was good for her.

'You'll be so much more ready to take on the very strenuous exercises they'll expect you to do at the Centre, if you have these months in the sun first,' Miss Makepeace urged each morning, again each afternoon. She had never expected the opportunity of spending three months out of England, all expenses paid, to come her way. It was like suddenly winning the pools. And now this joy was to be snatched from her, simply because this spoilt chit refused to leave home. Afraid of losing her boy friend, no doubt, Miss Makepeace, exasperated, commented waspishly one afternoon.

'Oh no,' Rosie said at once. 'It isn't Rupert who's keeping her here – he'd be going out with us. Didn't I tell you? I know the Alnakers expect him to stay for a fortnight at least, and then he's going to fly out for week-ends, too.'

Miss Makepeace was impressed. 'It must be most dreadfully expensive,' she ventured.

'Lady Alnaker intends to come for week-ends, too,' Rosie added proudly, delighted to be able to consider herself part of this privileged household. 'And I daresay even Lord Alnaker will manage to pop out once or twice.'

Miss Makepeace was unmistakably awed, and this made Rosie warm to her, feel she herself was sponsoring the physiotherapist in her first excursion into the rich world of lavish spending, idleness in the sun, *la dolce vita*. Rosie wasn't exactly comfortably at home there, of course. But it was pleasantly reassuring to pretend for a few minutes that this was her natural habitat, to be able to introduce and instruct the new girl. The result was that when Miss Makepeace's next question came, instead of snubbing her, Rosie found herself answering.

'Then why on earth,' Miss Makepeace had demanded, 'doesn't the silly girl want to go?'

'Something to do with that tiresome Toby Grant,' Rosie explained promptly – and of course, accurately. 'He's always had far too much influence over Julie, in my opinion. They used to play together as children, you see. I was against it from the beginning. After all, the Grants are *nobody*. But Lord Alnaker insisted. He and Grant served in the Western Desert together in the war.'

'But what would Toby Grant have to do with Julie's refusal to go to this villa?' Miss Makepeace persisted, puzzled.

'Everything, if I know Julie,' Rosie said crossly.

After Miss Makepeace had gone, she tackled Julie again. 'Simply because that inconsiderate Toby wanted you to go to this

129

Centre in Halchester, is not reason for ignoring the advice of everybody round you,' she said tartly. 'I think I may say we can be expected to know better than he does what will benefit you. No one who has your welfare at heart would want to see you travelling in and out daily, quite unnecessarily, to that Centre, which in any case is meant only for a rather common sort of person, Miss Makepeace tells me. Only someone like Toby would have dreamt of suggesting it for you – he has never had the slightest idea of what is owed to your position.'

There was no answer to this except in words that Rosie would undoubtedly – and correctly – have accused her of picking up from Toby, and Julie made none. But lying awake in the darkness that night – she was trying to manage without her sleeping tablets, since they interfered so much with her ability to do her exercises in the morning – she knew that her old governess's suspicions were well founded.

Ever since that day Toby had stormed in and bawled her out, she had entirely changed her attitude. Now she was possessed by the determination not only to lose weight fast, but to get to this dreadful Centre of which everyone so much disap-

proved, allow them to do their worst. She
was dead scared. But failure or success in
life, as far as she was concerned now, could
only be measured in terms of achievement
at the Rehabilitation Centre at St Mark's. It
was for this reason she was adamant in her
refusal to go to this villa on the shores of the
Adriatic. She knew, too, that to give in to her
mother now might be to give in for ever.
For, staring into the darkness, she admitted
that what was motivating her was not simply
the determination to regain her health. She
wanted more than anything else to escape
from her family's clutches, attain indepen-
dence, a life of her own. And this went back
a good deal further than the recent en-
counter with Toby, she thought. Right back
to that searing row they had had that
evening in the orangery, before she had ever
been engaged to Rupert, when Toby had
told her she had become no more than her
mother's puppet.

This illness had shown her what it meant
to be dependent on others. Never again.
Somehow she was going to free herself.
Battle on until she had become an independent adult in her own right.

So what about Rupert?

She pushed the unanswerable question

away. When she was fit and active again would be time enough to deal with that problem.

That Saturday Adam told her that before she could start at the Rehabilitation Centre she would have to be admitted again to St Mark's. She needed nearly a week of further tests, so that Adam and the neurologist could evaluate the progress she had so far made, the outlook for the future. This would decide what her programme of rehabilitation at the Centre should be.

In St Mark's Julie began to understand what Dr Buckland had been talking about when he had doubted her ability to stand the rigours of the National Health Service. This time – at her own insistence – she was neither in a private room nor in the intensive care unit. Simply in the orthopaedic ward. And within an hour or two she was fervently wishing herself back at home in the Gatehouse with Rosie, with the despised glass of sherry before lunch, the proffered menu, afternoon tea off the heavy silver tray with the delicate Minton china. No alcohol now, tea and coffee almost indistinguishable, slopping over into the saucer, lukewarm and weak in thick white cups. And although St Mark's was a hospital she gained a distinct impression that no one could have cared less whether she lived or died – except, that is, the patients on either side of her, who would undoubtedly have been worried stiff, would have certainly done their best to attract a nurse's attention on her behalf. She gritted her teeth and stuck it out. She wasn't going to climb down now, creep home to private treatment and Dr Buckland, followed by months abroad. She gritted her teeth for other reasons, too. The tests were numerous, long drawn-out, exhausting, often worrying and embarrassing. Many of the doctors and technicians carrying them out were absent-minded, off-hand, curt – overworked and preoccupied. Julie saw her individuality depart, felt herself lose all identity, become simply a series of results for Mr Trowbridge.

All day long, too, she recognized her appearance to be no more than a mess, and this was the most demoralizing factor of all. Untidy, tousled, her face shiny with sweat, her clothes pulled on anyhow – with her lower limbs unresponsive she was unable to dress herself successfully in the time she had available. Rosie had always managed for her.

No Rosie now. The nurses did in fact help her when they could spare time, but after all, they told her, she wasn't ill, was she? Only in for tests, so if she could cope it would be splendid. And, while before her illness she had always brushed her own hair, seen to her own make-up, recently she had fallen into the habit of allowing Miriam to do all this for her, so that now she had to do it for herself she felt flung together. Untidy, shabby, seedy. Confidence oozed stealthily away. With each test she was grubbier, her garments more awry, her hair increasingly dishevelled. Each day, when at last she found herself back in the ward, caught sight of herself in her hand mirror, she saw a bedraggled waif with pallid skin, collapsed hair, crumpled clothing.

Rupert, as ever, came in each evening at visiting time. Julie was ashamed to greet him. 'I'm sorry, Rupert, I know I look a total wreck,' she apologized.

'Of course not. You look super, darling. Simply super.' But he said it without conviction, merely because it was the right thing to say, and Julie read the truth in his shifting eyes.

Rupert had gone off her. She no longer attracted him in any way. Devoted, attentive, he came to see her as a duty only. It had taken her admission to St Mark's to make this apparent to her. This knowledge, she reminded herself, should have made matters simpler. But it didn't. Instead, it depressed her. Previously, meeting him alone, both of them cosily tucked away in the Gatehouse, she had made no comparisons, had seen her days through her own eyes only. Now, among strangers, watching other patients meeting their relatives and friends, for the first time she looked through Rupert's eyes.

She saw herself a poor thing. Depression washed over her. The truth was she had nothing to offer Rupert or Toby. Toby had gone, in any case, back to his own London life. But Rupert was caught here, trapped by an ailing, plaintive invalid.

She was right. Trapped was exactly how Rupert felt. Not only by Julie, either. By Veronica. Week by week, claustrophobia had crept insidiously through him, although at first, to be accepted as a son-in-law at Alnaker Hall had been the summit of his ambitions. Already, as a consequence of his Alnaker connection, he had been offered a junior partnership in his firm.

Surely, though, he loved Julie, didn't he? He had loved her once, he knew that. But then he had fallen for Veronica for a brief period, whereas now she terrified him. But Julie? In

135

all honesty, he had to admit to himself she no longer seemed the same girl. Those happy confident early days filled with joy and discovery had slipped like a dream into the past. Reality was a pale invalid, remote and frail – and on the pedantic side, too, if he was to be truthful, too intellectual and bookish for him. He could no longer imagine himself leading a normal married life with her.

What he wanted, in fact, was out.

But he could see no possibility of escape. He had to pull himself together, face up to his responsibilities, he reminded himself. He'd taken them on with his eyes open. And perhaps it would be different in this villa in the sun. Different, too, when Julie had come further along the path to recovery. Perhaps, in a few months, he'd be able to look back on his anxieties and see them as temporary, trivial. He and Julie might be happy and secure together once she was on her feet.

In the meantime they were all awaiting the results of the tests. Would she regain her full health? Most important of all, would she be able to leave her wheelchair, walk easily and freely again?

None of the doctors told Julie what they had found. They talked to each other, in an unintelligible jargon, but seldom to her, other than to say things like 'Keep still' or 'Now the other leg'. She had never grasped before that although money might not be able to buy any improvement in the standard of treatment, it certainly paid for extra time, for politeness and, apparently, the leisure to explain, comment, encourage. Wealth had cushioned her against the pressures of staff shortages, she saw, and she began to understand that she might indeed have been, as Miss Makepeace had so infuriatingly stated, leading a sheltered and protected existence.

On Friday, with the tests at last completed, she returned thankfully to the Gatehouse for a civilized lunch. Rosie came to the hospital for her in the Rolls, restored her smoothly to the comforts of home. She would not see Adam Trowbridge and the neurologist – who was coming down from London especially – until the following morning.

A thin, precise individual with steel-grey hair close to his head, formal pin-stripe suiting, Sir Arthur Gascoigne, the Central's Professor of Neurology, was angular and spare beside the stocky Adam – who, though he usually wore a light-weight suit for his week-end clinic at St Mark's, had donned the regulation sombre pin-stripe himself, in honour of the eminent neurologist. Simon

Keeble, too, had climbed into his darkest and most recently-acquired formal suit for the occasion, had at first worn his teaching hospital tie. But he was an Anselm's man, while Gascoigne had never been kindly disposed to outsiders, as he considered them. So on second thoughts Simon had substituted his university tie. He and Sir Arthur had both been to Cambridge, at least. His registrar, he saw, was wearing an Anselm's tie. Well, it couldn't be helped now, and he was thankful to see he'd the sense to put on a white shirt instead of the lurid purple job he'd worn so much recently.

Sir Arthur Gascoigne normally didn't give a thing away, but even his jaw could be seen to drop a little when the Alnaker party showed up.

Julie had had more than enough of looking a wreck, so that morning Miriam had done her hair for her, had arranged it high on the crown of her head, had done her make-up too. As a result Julie knew herself considerably better prepared for the day, and Sir Arthur and Adam found themselves confronted by a poised and lacquered beauty in a wheelchair, a mink coat draped casually round her shoulders, flanked by another stunning triumph of the beautician's and couturier's arts. Veronica, also hung with mink. These two fashion plates were attended by an unmistakable lady-in-waiting, a misleadingly gentle soul in soft tweeds, pushing the wheelchair. Rosie.

The scene that ensued, though it began conventionally enough, was to take them all by surprise. After Adam had performed the initial introductions, Sir Arthur embarked on a routine formula.

'Now, Miss Alnaker, as you know, I've been looking at the results of these tests you've been having during the past week. What I propose to do first of all is just to run through them with you.' Julie didn't, of course, recognize it, but here lay the explanation of the refusal of any junior doctor to attempt to discuss the tests with her. The Professor of Neurology from London would undoubtedly have his own interpretations, and none of them was going to blot his copybook in advance. 'I shall explain what they show, each of them, exactly what they're going to mean to you as far as your future mobility and your way of life are concerned. I expect you'd like your mother to remain with you while we discuss this, wouldn't you?' A mere formality, this, he didn't pause even, had begun the next sentence before he heard the clear 'No' that had so startlingly emanated from the patient.

Six pairs of eyes swivelled.

'No, thank you,' Julie said.

'But Julie dear, surely...' Rosie, predictably, began to fuss.

'What on *earth* do you mean, for heaven's sake?' Veronica easily drowned Rosie's twitter.

'Er – do I – um – understand you to say, Miss Alnaker, that – er – you...' Sir Arthur, for once fluffing his lines, at a loss.

Simon Keeble in the background blew his nose vigorously, while his registrar and staff nurse might have been watching tennis. Eyes left, eyes right, eyes left again.

Adam grasped the nettle. 'Want to talk to us alone, without Lady Alnaker or Miss Penrose, do you, Julie?' he asked briskly.

'Of course she doesn't,' Veronica responded irritably.

'I don't really think ... Julie, I'm sure you weren't intending, were you, dear, that...' Rosie was hot with embarrassment and alarm. What *was* she to do?

'Because of course you can, if that's what you'd like,' Adam continued unperturbed.

'Yes, please,' Julie said with the same bell-like clarity as before. She was a little pink in the face, Adam saw, but clearly immovable. In one of her obstinate moods, as Rosie easily recognized.

'Then of course you shall.' Sir Arthur regained control. 'We can all have a discussion a little later on. In the meantime, Lady Alnaker, if you and Miss Er would be so kind as to wait – nurse, would you mind – thank you so much.' The staff nurse opened the door and ushered an agitated, trembling Rosie through it. 'Ten minutes or so, shall we say, Lady Alnaker, if you would be good enough...' Sir Arthur was no slouch himself when it came to handling relatives, and he took the mink-encased arm in a firm grip and walked the seething – and astonished – Veronica out of the corridor. 'Nurse will you find somewhere comfortable to sit,' he announced. With totally misplaced confidence, as it happened. But this was not a problem that crossed the threshold of his attention. All he was interested in was removing the unwanted bodies from his consulting room.

He shut the door on Veronica's outrage, and turned to Julie, making a rapid reassessment of the situation. 'Now, young woman,' he began, on a more down-to-earth note than he'd employed previously, 'What was that in aid of?'

CHAPTER EIGHT

Rupert

The architectural partnership of Armitage & Waldron was housed in one of the original Georgian terraces in Bloomsbury, built in 1720 to house the newly prospering businessmen from the City of London, an easy carriage drive to the east. The derelict interior, worm-eaten and damp, had been stripped out, and the building today was radiant with light and air, a spiral staircase soaring dizzily upwards to the drawing office under the huge skylights in the roof.

Kenneth Waldron, tall, thin, stooping, untidy-haired and more reminiscent of an absent-minded poet than the busy, practical architect he in fact was, received Max in his room on the first floor, where, in what had been a spacious drawing-room two hundred years ago, tall eighteenth-century sash windows caught the morning sun. He rose to greet his visitor, though, from a desk that was very much of the twentieth-century.

Rosewood and steel, filing drawers on ball-bearings and a battery of telephones and dictating machines. He established Max in one of the soft black leather chairs by the low coffee table under the windows, offered drinks. The Alnaker Hall contract was important to the Halchester branch of the partnership, while the London office had been responsible for the alterations to the Alnaker house in Park Lane. Waldron would cheerfully have gone to see Max in his own office – or, indeed, anywhere else, New York or Cape Town, if he'd suggested it.

But he hadn't proposed anything of the kind. He had said he'd like to come round, and round he came, accepted a drink, sat back, chatted as though he had all day to spare. In fact he had a bare half-hour free, had sandwiched this call between two appointments – one at Scotland Yard, where, though Max himself remained sceptical, they seemed to believe an attempt was going to be made to steal the Nicholas Hilliard miniatures from the Hall, and another at the Bank of England for a committee on exchange control.

However, apparently unconscious of time, he sat back discussing the proposed conversion of the cottages at the Hard into a hotel – Veronica's latest enthusiasm – and so, by almost imperceptible stages, reached Rupert Ferris and his work.

The stages, though, had been far from imperceptible to Waldron, from the outset highly suspicious. What was it Lord Alnaker had come to say? Why had he chosen to visit the Great Charles Street premises? If he had wanted to talk about the cottages at the Hard, or the dry rot in the portico, he might have been expected to do it down at the Hall itself. Something was up. Had he been having trouble with Rupert? Was that blasted boy, far from binding it to the firm with bonds of cast iron, actually going to lose them the lucrative Alnaker contract? It began to seem appallingly likely.

'He's had a difficult time recently, of course,' Max was saying. 'With my daughter's illness and so on. It hasn't been easy for him.'

Waldron shivered inwardly. Exactly as he had feared. Rupert had boobed.

He was right, of course.

The trouble had been unearthed by Rosie, of all people. And it had only been because Miss Makepeace had upset her that Rupert's perfidy (Rosie's term, needless to say) had been discovered at all. One morning, after leaving Julie at the Rehabilitation Centre,

144

Rosie had driven on into Halchester, parked the car – a Saab estate car from the Hall pool – gone into the Copper Kettle to meet Miss Makepeace. They sat down cosily together at a table in the window, overlooking the High Street, ordered the excellent coffee that the Copper Kettle provided, chose home-made cakes.

At this point Miss Makepeace had dropped her brick. 'I suppose you hardly know what to do with yourself now that Miss Alnaker is at the Rehabilitation Centre all day,' she had volunteered sympathetically. Unfortunately, though, she was at least the tenth person to make the comment, and, worse still, she had hit the nail bang on the head. Rosie had time on her hands. What was she going to do with herself in future? She wished she knew.

After Miss Makepeace departed to her next case, Rosie was left facing once again the bleak knowledge that there was now no job for her at the Hall. She had allowed herself to be ousted from the post of Veronica's secretary, and as a result there was nothing left for her to do. At fifty-two, she might one day find herself not only out of work but homeless. Demoralized and miserable, she left the Saab in the car park, walked towards the Cathedral. A stroll in these quiet precincts might steady her nerves, she hoped, even bring her some sort of reassurance. For here she had a place still. Here, as a child, she had often come with her father, and though the dean who remembered Canon Penrose had long since retired, they continued to invite her regularly to the Deanery for clergy teas. Perhaps she could find a post in the offices attached to the Cathedral, if all else failed, she thought, wandering slowly on, eventually, on her way back to the car park, taking the path between the Chapter House and the Canonry. And here, tucked away in the Canons' Garden, on a seat by the lily pond, sat Samantha and Rupert, their heads close as they talked earnestly and emphatically.

Rosie was shocked. Although she had never particularly liked Rupert, she had believed implicitly in his devotion to Julie. So what was he doing here with Samantha?

Worried, now, not about herself at all but about Julie, she collected the Saab, drove anxiously out of the town. What ought she to do? Tell Julie what she had seen? Or remain silent?

Not until she was approaching the Hall did it strike her that her own problems could be over. She had merely to tell Veronica what she had seen. That would be the end of Samantha.

Veronica was more irritated than anything else when Rosie broke the news. 'Neither of them told *me,*'she said crossly. 'I really think it's rather peculiar of both of them.' As she thought it over, she became increasingly indignant, and greeted Max with the story as soon as he came down at the week-end. 'Samantha must go,' she said. 'She can't be trusted any more. I don't know what she gets up to behind my back.'

Her departure might even be something of a relief, though Veronica concealed this aspect of the situation. At first, she had found it stimulating to have this charming young creature helping her in the office. She had an efficient secretary at last, decorative too, who could be relied on to grace any social occasion, play assistant hostess as competently as she made appointments and typed letters. Veronica's days, hardworking always, went at a rapid gallop after Samantha took over from Rosie.

But Veronica had never been accustomed to living at this pace, nor to having most of her decisions made for her. Her self-importance took a knock. What she was used to, after all, was the dependence and amiable muddling about of dear old Rosie. To be without this had to begin with been a pleasure, but Veronica wasn't at all sure she wouldn't be thankful to have her back again.

'As Julie's going to be away all day at that wretched Centre, I can use Rosie again in the office, and get rid of Samantha,' Veronica told Max. 'Dear old thing, it *will* be nice to have her back.'

Max couldn't have cared less what Veronica did about Samantha or Rosie. He was worried about Julie. He had an excellent intelligence service, when he chose to tap it, down at the Hall as well as in the City, and soon elicited the facts. What Rosie had stumbled on had not been a single isolated incident. Everyone but the family had apparently known for months that Samantha and Rupert were in the habit of meeting frequently.

Rumour, not for the first time, had added two and two, made twenty-two. There was no secret affair between Rupert and Samantha – indeed, though she kept this to herself, Samantha thought him a bit of a wet. Their meetings were not assignations at all, simply an attempt to form a trade union, a get-together by rebellious and dissident staff, and their conversation was apt to be concerned

148

with the tiresomeness of Veronica, how over-bearing she was (Rupert), how unpredictable and contrary her demands (Samantha). But because both of them had come up against her possessiveness more than once, they had agreed that to mention their meetings to her would be asking for trouble. Unfortunately, of course, the secrecy led in the end to even greater trouble, for Max was convinced by this, as well as by what he heard from staff and friends, as he had not been by Rosie's own report.

He was in a quandary. This was no time, in his opinion, for Rupert to be playing around with pretty blondes almost on the doorstep. But what was he to do?

Like any sensible father, he decided to play for time. Julie must in the end decide for herself about her own marriage. He'd have to tell her what was being said about Rupert. But not yet. Once she'd come through the Rehabilitation Centre would be soon enough to ask her to face this new issue.

Meanwhile, emergency measures must be taken, Julie's peace of mind safeguarded. Hence his visit to Kenneth Waldron, who was immensely relieved to ascertain, reading carefully between the lines, that matters were not as bad as he had at first supposed.

It seemed that all Lord Alnaker required him to do was to remove Rupert temporarily from the scene. As soon as he grasped this, he cheered up, promptly offered Max, in his turn, a few lines to read between.

'We've a big contract in Nigeria going to keep us busy for the next five years or so.' Meandering amiably and deviously along architectural byways, groaning over problems of keeping labour in Africa, the installation of air conditioning plant and its maintenance, the necessity for tropicalization of all equipment, the slowness of supplies, the uncertainty of shipping lines, he at last reached the point at which he'd been aiming. 'As you can guess, there's a fair amount of detail which needs to be handled on the spot. I'd like to keep a man out there from now on,' he said. 'Excellent experience for a young architect, of course. If he hadn't been rather tied to Halchester recently, I'd have liked Rupert to take it on. I'm beginning to wonder, though, if it isn't an opportunity we ought to offer him. What would you feel about it, I wonder, if I put one of my assistants in the Halchester office for the next few months, and took Rupert with me to Lagos in ten days? Left him out there to handle that end for a while? Would it be asking too much?'

On the contrary, Max assured him, Rupert had his career to think of, must on no account miss chances like this. No one, least of all the Alnaker family, would wish him to do anything of the sort. He'd speak to his daughter about it, was sure, though, she'd understand and agree entirely. Then, too, she was going to be very fully occupied herself for the next few months at the Rehabilitation Centre in Halchester. 'After that we can see,' he added.

Everything became clear. The Alnakers were about to drop Rupert Ferris. There wasn't, in Waldron's opinion, going to be any Alnaker-Ferris wedding. But if he, Waldron, played his cards carefully, kept his head, sent Rupert to Nigeria – and kept him there for the next five years if necessary – he might well salvage the Alnaker contract.

When he heard about Nigeria, Rupert was pleased that Waldron had, as he innocently imagined, chosen him for this responsible assignment. On the whole, too, he was thankful to be able to escape from Veronica and the Hall for a brief period, sort his ideas out. All that remained was to break the news to Julie, and about this he was uneasy. Would she feel he was abandoning her? He soon discovered, though, that she already knew about his trip, was urging him to accept the offer. 'You can't possibly miss an opportunity like this, simply because of me,' she told him.

A weight was lifted, Rupert's spirits rose, he was light-hearted as he hadn't been for months. 'Come out for a celebration dinner tomorrow, darling,' he suggested in his relief, the plan taking him as much by surprise as it did Julie.

She turned towards him in her wheelchair, her eyes startled. 'But,' she began, 'I don't know how I'd–'

'We'd manage,' Rupert asserted. At this precise moment his confidence had never been higher. He would have offered to push down mountains, had it been required. 'After tomorrow, I'll have to be in London, having my briefing about this Nigerian job, seeing about my jabs and so on. Do say you'll come. After all, if Rosie can take you into Halchester every day, surely I can take you out for one evening?'

Julie's reactions were chaotic. Suddenly Rupert was looking at her in the old way, and it was undeniably warming. More than that. Exciting. She had told herself that everything between them was over, yet now it seemed as if they might be on the brink of reaching a new understanding. Was this what she wanted? Or not? She couldn't tell.

One fact, though, stood out. Rupert was making a tremendous effort. She must at least go half-way to meet him.

'Super,' she agreed. 'Let's do that.'

Rupert was beginning to see that he ought to have made some attempt of this sort long before. What had stopped him? Why had he come regularly up here to the Gatehouse, had his glass of sherry with Julie, then cleared off obediently to consume a formal dinner with Veronica? What had possessed him to allow Veronica to rule him, as she had undoubtedly been doing? He wanted to make it all up to Julie, to take her out, make a tremendous fuss of her, get her away from the Hall, Veronica, Rosie, be alone with her at last.

'Do you realize,' he asked her excitedly, 'we haven't been out together since last autumn?'

'It seems like several years ago,' Julie said pensively and, Rupert decided, more than a little forlornly.

'We'll have a terrific celebration,' he told her. Once again he longed to cherish her, protect her, look after her. She was his darling Julie, she was going to make a complete recovery, they'd marry and be happy. 'We'll go to the Blue Boar,' he suggested. 'I'll book a table for tomorrow night.'

'Lovely,' Julie agreed.

The next evening, though, when she returned from the Rehabilitation Centre, she longed only to be able to lie on her bed, sleep for ever. She had completed nearly three weeks at the Centre, though she had never been so tired in her life.

Determined not to give in, not to allow herself to back out of the dinner engagement, she went to the house telephone, dialled the hairdresser. 'Miriam? Julie here.'

Miriam nearly dropped the instrument. For months now, Julie's appointments had been made by Rosie. 'Is that the hairdresser?' she would invariably begin. 'Ah. Thank you. Yes. This is Miss Penrose from the Gatehouse. Miss Alnaker would like her hair done in half an hour.' Now, though, it was back to 'Miriam? Julie here,' as it had been in the old days.

'Want me to come over?' Miriam inquired.

'Well, I'm going out to the Blue Boar for dinner–'

'Blue Boar. How fab.'

'All I hope is I can get there and back without falling out of my chair or making a

154

fool of myself. But I'm going to change now, so could you come over and give me a comb out in about an hour?'

'That'll be fine. I'll be over. Want me to do your face for you, too?'

Julie chuckled. 'It'll look a lot better if you do. And I'd say it could do with that.' She grimaced, unseen, at her pale, exhausted reflection.

'O.K. I'll be along.'

When Miriam arrived, Julie was in her chair, wearing the trousers of her black velvet pants suit and waiting for Miriam to fasten her frivolous lacy shirt with its rows of tiny buttons down the centre of the back. Rosie had always disliked the black velvet suit, had hidden the outfit away at the back of a cupboard, and Julie had had some trouble in locating it.

'Hi,' Miriam announced herself. 'You look great.'

'I feel whacked,' Julie admitted. 'Much more ready for total collapse than for an evening at the Blue Boar, I'm afraid. Getting changed has been about as strenuous as dancing all night would have been at one time.' She pulled a face. 'I daresay I'll survive.'

'I reckon a strong gin would help you on

your way,' Miriam suggested. Unlike Rosie, who thought it a vulgar drink, Miriam was a believer in gin for uplift.

'Let's both have a gin.' Julie agreed. She didn't in fact much care for the stuff, but she had had more than enough of Rosie's dry sherry in cut-glass. This evening at least gin spelled emancipation.

Miriam poured generous slugs into tumblers, added tonic and ice, brought Julie her glass. 'You do look a bit frail, I must say,' she told her. 'But make-up will hide it. Now, how do you want your hair?'

When Rupert arrived, he was over-whelmed. There once again was the girl he had fallen in love with, huge-eyed, beautiful, in black velvet and frothing lace, slim and lovely, waiting for him. For the first time, her wheelchair, instead of frightening him away, added to her appeal for him by stressing her continuing need for his protection.

For both of them the evening passed in a daze. A daze of love and joy for Rupert, of fatigue and exhaustion for Julie. The Blue Boar – all of whose meals were renowned locally – provided one of their most superb menus, made an enormous fuss. They knew exactly whom they were serving, of course. The Blue Boar seldom slipped up on detail.

Lord Alnaker's only daughter, who had had that tragic accident last year, and, if they were not mistaken, was making her first public appearance since the disaster. In a wheelchair. In their restaurant. And with her future husband, who – if all the stories about the Hon. James Alnaker were to be believed – might well be marrying the heiress to the Alnaker fortune.

Rupert enjoyed the attention they received. Most of all, though, he enjoyed Julie. In the oak-panelled restaurant with the crimson tablecloths and glittering chandeliers, opposite him Julie in black velvet and lace ruffles, diamonds sparkling at her ears, on her lapel – his own diamond on her finger – her hair piled darkly above the pale forehead, the wide mouth he loved crinkling into a smile he knew was meant only for him, he vowed to himself that he would remain true to her for ever.

Nigeria would be interesting, of course, and a break from Veronica would be more than welcome. He could do with that. An interval, too, to concentrate once again on work, free from the Hall and its incessant demands. Afterwards, though, the sure return to Julie, to begin their life together. Over his wine glass, he looked at her longingly. She was so beautiful, and he loved her so much. This accident, after all, had only temporarily interfered with their marriage plans.

'When I come back from Nigeria,' he promised her, 'it'll all be as it was before. You'll be strong again, able to get about as we used to do. We can begin thinking about the future.'

Julie looked vaguely back at him. That evening everything reached her through a blue of fatigue. Even so, his love and admiration, to be enfolded in this joyous confidence, was surprisingly uplifting. Rupert was to be her husband, over a year ago she had promised to marry him. He was faithful and enduring. What more could she ask? Why for all these months had she allowed her thoughts of Toby to come between them? It wasn't even as if Toby had any interest in her, either. He'd simply been kind – and so gentle – while she had been ill. But then that was, after all, his job. And he'd soon stopped being gentle, too. The moment she'd left the hospital he'd returned to his usual impatient, outspoken bluntness.

Like so many silly patients before her, she'd built a fairy story round Toby, made him into her Prince Charming. But this must have been simply a passing madness, born in the hot-house atmosphere of an intensive care ward, and meaningless in real life. Through a mist of invading fatigue, she saw Rupert watching her. Admiring her. Attentive. Real life, she reminded herself, was marriage with Rupert.

Only was it? Which was the dream, which the reality? Julie, looking at Rupert but once again seeing Toby, was too exhausted to attempt to work it out.

CHAPTER NINE

Halchester Rehabilitation Centre

Real life was going to the Centre five days a week, returning exhausted, swallowing her evening meal, looking at a book or a magazine with her eyes beginning to close. Off to the Centre again in the morning, for another day of arduous activity. Her day at the Centre became all that mattered to Julie. Absorbed in her progress there, the Hall and its concerns receded into the background. The patients at the Centre shared triumph and failure with her, just as she shared their achievements and disasters. This now was the meaning of her days.

She'd shed Rosie, too, was no longer a privileged outsider, arriving by car, as she'd been in the beginning. 'Is there any chance that the ambulance that collects the others could pick me up?' she had inquired one day during her first week. 'Or would it be out of the way?'

'They go to Alnaker St Nicholas in any

case, for old Mrs Hodgson. I should think they could easily pick you up on the way.'

So it was arranged. Julie enjoyed herself with the patients in the ambulance, a cheery, matey lot, whose gossiping friendliness made an entertaining opening to the hardworking regime of the Centre. In age they were a mixed bunch. Old Mrs Hodgson from the little sweetshop and sub-post office at Alnaker St Nicholas Julie had known all her life, though never before as well as now. Three months earlier Mrs Hodgson had had a stroke. Now she was trying to walk again, with a tripod, learning to use her weakened left hand, too. Meanwhile her daughter-in-law – a mere girl of sixty-odd – had to deal with the housekeeping and help out in the shop as well. Mrs Hodgson was keen to make progress, return to run the shop again. She was Julie's contemporary as far as admission to the Centre went – all they any of them thought about – and vied with her, as they tottered along together on their walking frames, their knees apt to buckle under them, their control of direction erratic. 'I'll be beating you in the hundred yards sprint yet, Julie, see if I don't,' Mrs Hodgson boasted, with the chuckle that Julie remembered so well from sweet-buying expeditions throughout her childhood.

Then there was young Barry Fripp in his chair. No chance of Barry walking again, he'd been too badly wrecked in an accident on the motorway two years earlier. But he enjoyed the company at the Centre, liked to join in the games of throwing and catching with the stroke patients – who all made a tremendous fuss of him – and, in addition, he was learning to work a machine in the carpentry room. The usual objective there was to prepare patients for the Industrial Rehabilitation Unit, where they could learn a new trade, but Barry, everyone knew, would never get as far as this.

The Rehabilitation Centre at St Mark's shared premises and staff with the Day Centre run by the Old People's Welfare Association, and for some it was the last staging post before leaving home and entering the geriatric wards. Some of them were, in the eyes of the staff, 'dear old pets' for whom no one could do enough. Others were eccentric, odd, often out of touch and difficult to manage, as apt to undress or make a pool at precisely the most inconvenient moment as any two-year-old. They were amazingly well tolerated by their fellow patients, who were often able to catch them in the nick of time. Old Mrs Catchpole, for instance, liked to don her knickers as a sunbonnet. It was a signal. If received and interpreted fast, she could be enticed to the cloakrooms before too late. Julie had never had to deal with old people like this before, and at first she was at a loss, unable to communicate with them, and as a result dead scared of them.

In fact, she was dead scared for much of the day. Of falling over, most of all. The head physiotherapist at the Centre, Diana Lawford, was as about as unlike Miss Makepeace as anyone could be. She was a slight, apparently dreamy blonde with fly-away hair, her appearance suggesting she could be pushed around by anyone who felt in the mood. This was a misleading impression, in practice she was a good deal tougher than Miss Makepeace, and assumed Julie was well able to prance round the department clutching only what seemed to her a rickety walking frame or using elbow crutches threatening to slide out at wild angles like the skis of a novice on the slopes at St Moritz or Mürren. To Julie all floors these days were as glassy and potentially lethal as an ice-rink. Her legs were not her own to command, and if she broke a limb she'd be strung up in plaster for months. She didn't feel she could bear to go through yet another period of hospitalisation, followed inevitably by dependence on Rosie again.

'What are you so frightened of?' Diana demanded.

'Everything,' Julie had to admit. 'Falling over most of all, I suppose. I seem to have no control at all. Anything could happen.'

One morning, tired of this, Diana suddenly stopped all her exercises and activities. No throwing games with the stroke patients, no table tennis in her wheelchair against Barry in his. Diana put her into a crash helmet and made her practice falling. Nothing else. 'If you can't lose this feeling of panic each time you are unsteady, you'll never get anywhere. And it's absolutely vital you should stay out of your chair. On two sticks if you have to, but upright. *Upright,* duckie. Understand? Otherwise you're inviting all sorts of consequences. Kidney disease, infections, the lot.'

Julie, puffing and unnerved, begged at least to be allowed to take it more slowly.

'No.' Diana was adamant. 'Come on, Julie. You've got to bash away at it. Look at old Mrs Hodgson, in her eighties, struggling along in her walking frame. She's not afraid of falling over. You ought to be ashamed of yourself. You're only a quarter of her age, and you've got your health and strength, too.'

'I've got my *what* did you say?' Julie gasped.

'Your health and strength, I said,' Diana bawled. 'You have, you know. By the standards of most people here you're *fit,* Julie. All you've got is a bit of residual disability.'

A bit of residual disability. That was how they saw it at the Centre. Julie had been thinking herself crippled for life.

'You've some muscular weakness, of course,' Diana went on bracingly. 'As well as a few neurological complications that leave you a bit unsteady on your pins just now. But once you're used to being on your feet you'll soon learn to compensate. You'll begin to use different muscles, different nerves, from the ones you used before you had your accident. That's all. You'll soon find there's nothing to it.'

Nothing to it. Her muscles screamed agony. She was weak, unco-ordinated, her legs wobbled and refused to obey her. She was frightened, she frequently felt sick, nearly always tired. It was the hardest job in the world to learn to walk again. And when she wasn't falling about all over the place, Diana expected her to whiz round at horrific speed in the battery-powered chair she'd obtained for her, racing Barry. She encouraged her, too, to join in an exciting but extraordinarily alarming game played from wheelchairs in teams, a version of polo using upended walking sticks and a beach ball.

In spite of the fact, though, that she was terrified all day long, often exhausted and near to tears – more than once she lapsed into incoherence and sniffles – she was undoubtedly also happy. Each hour was filled with activity, she was in touch with her companions, no longer cut off from the world.

Toby's advice, in fact, had worked. In a sudden flashback to the moment when he had appeared, walking across the rose garden towards her as she sat in the orangery, she knew she had been alive then, too. She had come alive for Toby. Because of his presence, the air had glittered with promise and expectancy. A promise that had been fulfilled.

She remembered something else. Toby had told her she ought to arrange for a car to be converted, drive herself in it. She began to wonder. After all, why not? At the Centre she was learning to walk, trying not to be dependent on her wheelchair. But at the present rate of progress it would be months before she achieved this. All she could manage yet was to stumble across a room on elbow crutches. And she knew from what Adam Trowbridge and Sir Arthur Gascoigne had said that she was never again going to experience the easy freedom of movement that had been hers before the accident. Walking would always in future be a deliberate effort, and she would no longer be a stranger to pain. So why not drive herself, attain freedom at the wheel of a car?

On Saturday she went in search of Jo Grant, Toby's father. And it was like being reunited with Toby. There was the long square chin, the wide humorous mouth, the startling blue eyes. Jo's hair was grey, where Toby's was fair, but both of them had the same exuberant curls, though Jo's had been disciplined by stricter and shorter cutting than Toby's had ever undergone. But this, Julie saw with a pang, was almost exactly how Toby would look in thirty years' time, and at that moment she knew beyond any doubt that she wanted to remain alongside him throughout those years. She pushed this awkward and overwhelming reaction into a far corner of her mind, to be taken out and examined privately, explained to Jo

167

what she needed.

'Yes,' he said. 'Toby did mention you might be wanting something of the sort, so I've been thinking about it off and on. And what it seems to me is, you couldn't do much better than use the Saab estate car. That's the vehicle Miss Penrose was using to drive you to and from the Centre to begin with, you'll remember. You got your chair into the back of it easily enough, didn't you?'

Julie agreed.

'Though I hear you go in each day in the ambulance now, along with old Mrs Hodgson.'

'That's right.'

'And how's she getting on down there? According to what Jim Hodgson says, she comes home tired out, just about fit to crawl into bed, he told me. That hardly seems right, an old lady her age.' He scratched his curly head dubiously. The gesture might have been Toby.

'Just how I feel each day. They're slave-drivers there, Jo. But they seem to get results.'

'Finding it hard going, are you, then?'

Julie nodded.

The blue eyes surveyed her, summed her up. 'All I can say is, you look fighting fit on it. Colour in your cheeks, full of bounce.

168

Want to have a look at the Saab?'

They went to look at it, and Julie was able to show off satisfactorily by getting in and out of the driver's seat unaided. Jo praised her, though secretly he was appalled. This was Julie, whom he had known as a quick-silver child. At least, though, her morale was high.

'That's nothing,' she was assuring him. 'Next week I'm going to learn how to put the chair in as well as myself and get us both out again – though according to them I shan't be using the chair much in future. They're having me on elbow crutches first, and then two sticks.' She pulled a face. 'I find it all rather terrifying, I must say. But if Mrs Hodgson can make it, so can I.'

'That's the style. You keep at it. I'll arrange for this job to go to be converted for you – probably it'll take about a fortnight, I shouldn't wonder. There'll be no holding you then, I daresay. You'll be able to go any-where, do anything.' He grinned cheerfully, patted her encouragingly.

'How's Toby?' Julie asked abruptly.

'Bit cast down, poor laddie.'

'Oh, *why?*' Julie was jolted. Cast down? *Toby?*

'Seems they've broken it to him at the

169

hospital that they've not much use for him on the medical side, told him to get back to surgery. And of course he'd set his heart on medicine, as you know.'

'But *why* don't they want him?' Julie, furious, could hardly believe it. Not want *Toby?*

'Asked him that myself. He says he's not academic enough for them. According to him, they're all a lot of intellectual whiz kids on the medical unit, and he admits he can't compete. Tells me he knows they're right, it's true he's better with his hands than his head. Fortunately they still seem to want him on the orthopaedic wards, so he's back off there at the beginning of the month. He'll be a junior registrar then, so that's a step up anyway.'

'I would have thought,' Julie said indignantly, 'if they're giving him a registrar's post at his teaching hospital, he must be doing rather well.' These days she was not without knowledge of hospital attitudes. 'Some people at St Mark's would be over the moon if they'd had half the posts Toby's had.'

'Is that so? You might try telling him that, Julie. Because there's no doubt the boy's had a bit of a knock. He's making the best of it, of course, but then Toby always does put a good face on setbacks. He says he's glad to have had the medical experience, if only to find out at first hand that it wasn't for him. Asserts he felt like a carthorse confronted with the Grand National course. I think he must be exaggerating there, though.'

'Of course he must be.'

Frowning, her mind far from her own problems now, Julie turned her chair in the direction of the Gatehouse, bowled back along the paths and through the courtyard.

The week-end was full. Veronica had one of her ghastly house parties, while there was a garden fête on Sunday afternoon, in aid of the Cathedral restoration fund. 'You must play your part, Julie,' Veronica told her. 'I know on week-day evenings you're too tired after your day at the Centre to help me out with visitors, but at the week-end it's different. I must be able to count on you. After all, I haven't Samantha any longer. She was a marvellous hostess at these functions, much more use than poor Rosie. Of course she had her faults too, who hasn't? But in some ways, and especially on occasions like this, I miss her badly.' Veronica, cheerfully gossiping away, her mind on Rosie's incompetence and the week-end ahead, suddenly recollected why Samantha had had to go, that Julie was supposed to know nothing of it. 'Have you heard from Rupert?' she asked sharply.

Julie was immediately infuriated out of all reason, wanted to snap back like an angry child. 'Mind your own business.' She wasn't at all in the mood to discuss Rupert, and was put out, too, at this unwelcome reminder that time was going by, and still she had not come to a decision about him.

'What are you going to do about him?' Veronica's voice rang out like a hideous echo.

'Do about him?' Julie echoed back, playing for time.

'Yes, *do* about him,' Veronica repeated with what she felt was justifiable maternal irritation. 'After all, you can't keep him dangling for ever, can you? Playing about down at this Centre you're so mad on, refusing to go to this villa your father found. When are you and Rupert going to get *married?* You seem perfectly fit again to me if you didn't insist on wearing yourself out every day at St Mark's. I can't see what's to stop you marrying and settling down sensibly.' The truth was that Veronica, bereft of Samantha and Rupert, was more scratchy than usual, finding funny old Rosie and this remote and absent-minded daughter far from adequate substitutes. However, at this point the two of them had been interrupted by the arrival of the first of the week-end guests, and Veronica lost all interest in family problems, became again the busy hostess.

The dinner party that evening, to her relief, went well, was late breaking up. Everything was set for another successful week-end, she decided, retaining Julie and Rosie for some last-minute instructions.

When Julie arrived back in the Gatehouse, it was well after midnight. She knew exactly what she was going to do. All day and throughout the evening the plan had been forming at the back of her mind. Manoeuvring herself in her chair out of the lift into her sitting-room, she picked up the telephone, asked for an outside line, dialled the Central London Hospital.

Before she had a chance to rehearse what she was going to say to him, she heard herself asking for Toby. Astonishingly, she was immediately through. *'Julie?'* he repeated, apparently overcome by incredulity. As well he might be. What on earth could she have been thinking of? She must surely have been out of her mind.

'I hope it's all right to ring you so late,' she apologized, fussed now. 'You're not busy or something, I mean? If so, I can–'

'No, it's fine. I've just finished my round, I've loads of time.'

'Oh. Oh, good. Well, you see, the thing was, I thought I'd – actually, I was talking to your father yesterday, and he said – at least, I thought–'

'How are you getting on at the Centre?' Toby cut through all this waffle.

Julie chuckled. Suddenly she was the old Julie he'd always known. 'Hell,' she said. 'Absolute hell. I can't think why I keep on going there. But I didn't ring you to talk about me. What I wanted to ask you–'

'But I want to hear about you. Tell me exactly what you're doing at the Centre.'

'Falling over, mainly. But never mind that. Listen, Toby, your father said–'

'But I do mind that. What do you mean, falling over? What have they–'

'Shut *up*, Toby. I rang up to talk about you, not me.' Julie shouted back at him. 'Your father said you were starting a new job.'

'Oh, that. Oh yes. Yes. I am.'

'You don't sound very pleased.'

'I am in a way,' he said cautiously.

'In what way?'

174

'Well, there are a number of different aspects.' He was standing on the landing outside the acute medical wards, staff passing and repassing all the time. 'It's rather difficult to explain, especially just now. You see–'

Julie picked up the note of embarrassment at once.

'Other people there?' she asked.

'On and off.'

'I see,' she said. 'When are you coming home again? Because–'

'When–? I don't know. I take over this new job next week-end, so that's out, in any case, and after that I don't know at all how I'll be placed. Rotas and so on. I'll be on the surgical side again, too. Less time off, more interruptions.'

'Shall I come up and see you, then?'

'Come up and–' His voice was filled with blank stupefaction.

Now it was Julie's turn to be embarrassed. She wished her words unsaid. What could have come over her? This entire conversation was dotty, in the first place, quite apart from the fact, since they seemed unable to stop interrupting one another, that it never got anywhere.

Suddenly, though, Toby came out with

several consecutive sentences. 'Yes,' he said firmly. 'Do come up and see me, Julie. I'd love that. When can you come? And how?'

'Your father's getting the Saab converted for me. But he said it would take about a fortnight, so I shan't have it next week-end, I don't suppose.'

'Come the one after, then. I'll try and fix some time off.'

'Then we can have a talk,' Julie was radiant. 'I want to hear all about your job.'

'And I want to hear all about the Centre. I shall expect you to be on your feet, not in that blasted chair, you know.'

'Well, I may be, so there. Yah boo.' Julie slammed the receiver down, stared at it shining-eyed.

In the Central London Hospital Toby replaced his receiver. 'And yah boo to you, too,' he informed it. A delighted grin began to spread, as he gathered up his papers, went whistling down the corridors.

CHAPTER TEN

Philip and Julie

A week went by. As usual, it was strenuous. Rewarding, too, for Julie at last learnt to use the elbow crutches with confidence. Now it was Saturday again, and she was asking Jo Grant about the Saab.

'They've promised it for Wednesday,' he told her. 'So I'll have it collected that afternoon for you.'

'Could I try it out the same evening, do you think?'

'Yes, of course, if you want to. If you don't feel it'll be too tiring for you, after a day at the Centre.'

Julie shook her head, spoke vehemently. 'It won't have to be,' she said. 'I can't wait to find myself at the wheel of a car again.' She was remembering, too, her journey to London to see Toby the following week-end. For the present, though, she was keeping this to herself, as she had an uneasy feeling that Jo might try to stop her, or at least insist on

177

providing her with a driver. 'That's a date, then,' she said briskly, bowled her chair off along the passages to the hairdressing salon for a shampoo and set. The appointment made her too late for lunch with Veronica and her latest batch of week-end visitors. Instead she consumed salad and yoghourt in the salon with Miriam, followed by Nescafé made with water boiled in her electric kettle.

Afterwards Julie went back to the Gatehouse to complete a task she was dreading. She had to write the difficult letter to Rupert that would end their engagement. Crutches on the floor beside her – she'd abandoned the wheelchair out of sight in the hall – she sat down on the big chesterfield in her sitting-room, wrote with the pad on her knee, began with the thought uppermost in her mind. She was getting better, was able to move around more freely, know that at last her life was in her own hands again, that with each week that went by she grew stronger and fitter. 'Now that I am so much better,' she wrote, 'I can understand something of what an unfair strain these past months must have been for you.' The next sentences proved far more difficult, but eventually she had it all down on paper, added a final word that she hoped might soften the impact of the final break. 'I shall always remember the happiness we had, and your companionship while I've been ill.' And that was the truth, she thought, stilted and formal though it might sound. She sealed the letter, stamped it, even put herself into the now-hated wheelchair in order to take it down to the post-box at the end of the drive.

That evening there was to be a big dinner party, with the Lord Lieutenant of the county and various other notabilities. Veronica was planning a big charity fashion show – to be organized by Mark Midwinter – in the picture gallery, which would be graced, she hoped, by royalty. Hence the presence of the Lord Lieutenant, traditionally entitled to receive royalty who put so much as a toe into his county. Julie had promised to talk to him about the Alnaker pictures after dinner. 'You're so much better on them than I am,' Veronica assured her, giving credit where credit was due, but moving rapidly on to criticism of her daughter's latest hair style, together with detailed instructions on what she was to wear.

However, the dinner party went off well, the Lord Lieutenant was duly impressed by the gallery and the proposed arrangements for the reception of royalty, the plans for the fashion show were clinched with Mark Midwinter, and Veronica retired to bed at two in the morning well pleased with her family, for once. Even Rosie was in favour, having coped splendidly all evening with that dreadful old bore, the Lord Lieutenant's widowed sister.

Sunday dawned sunny and bright, a considerable relief to the staff, since that afternoon the gardens were to be opened for the Red Cross. Half the county poured in, Veronica wore her latest Mark Midwinter creation, an Edwardian confection in cream muslin with lace insertions, a high pin-tucked collar and full sleeves gathered into long tight cuffs with tiny buttons. She had a huge hat crowned with cream roses, and carried the parasol that had belonged to the Edwardian Lady Alnaker, Max's famous grandmother, the Jewish beauty who had brought both wealth and financial genius into the hitherto impoverished family.

Julie had agreed to establish herself in the rose garden with her guitar, had invited Mrs Hodgson to join her there. They intended to improve the shining hour by trying out a number of songs Julie was to play at the Centre during the lunch hour one day the following week. Because it was easy to put on and she felt comfortable in it, she wore a loose caftan in a dark jungle print of which both Veronica and Rosie disapproved. To less prejudiced eyes she appeared coolly elegant, slim and almost ethereal with her dark hair and pale skin, the air of exhausted fragility that seldom left her now. The visitors, at any rate, thought she made a charming picture, cheerfully paid the extra contribution demanded for entrance to the rose garden and orangery, together with a glass of ice-cold Moselle. Heavenly, they told one another, to be able to wander at leisure among the roses, heavy with scent, petals dropping in the sultry summer afternoon, drinking a delicious wine and listening to the soft chords produced by Lord Alnaker's pretty young invalid daughter – Julie, most unwillingly, had been forced to use the wheelchair that afternoon, not having been able to work out any method of managing two crutches and a guitar.

Among the visitors a tall young man in a grey lounge suit watched Julie over the rim of his glass. He made no attempt, however, to introduce himself, instead sought out Veronica. She stood in the centre of a group on the terrace, pink geraniums spilling from an urn beside her, setting off to perfection, as she was well aware, the cream of her dress and her dark glowing beauty. She noticed the young man standing on the fringe of her circle, liked what she saw. Attractive, she thought. Presentable, too. A good suit. She gave him a half smile, and, as she had known it would be, it was enough. He began to edge forward. Veronica decided to give him some help. 'We met somewhere,' she suggested, with the sensational smile that had once been her trademark. 'Now where was it? I'm afraid I can't for the moment quite place…'

'No, I'm afraid we didn't,' the young man said, with startling honesty. 'I wish we had.'

Veronica smiled delightedly. Not only charming, but unpretentious. 'Well,' she said, 'now we have done. So please introduce yourself.'

'Philip Slade,' he told her. 'I was in Bangkok recently – oh, several months ago now, it must be. Simply a brief stop-over between flights. But I met your son James, and he said if I was ever in this part of the world I was to be sure to look you up, so–'

'You know *James?*' Veronica was gripped instantly. 'How was he?'

'Very well indeed.'

'In Bangkok, you say?'

'Well, yes, but I think he was only passing through, as I was myself. On his way back to Nepal, I believe he said.'

Veronica nodded, kept Philip Slade by her side, took him with her to the select tea party for local V.I.P.s in the drawing room, invited him to stay on for dinner.

Max left for Park Lane before the meal, and took several of the guests with him, while others had already departed, so that it was a small, informal party that remained. Old Lady Inchmory, the dowager Countess, who was county President of the Red Cross, and a thorn in Veronica's side from time immemorial, her son-in-law and daughter, Lord and Lady Pedmore, Sir John Halford from Halford Place, and Dr Buckland and his wife. Veronica, who found them all thoroughly stuffy, heavy in the hand, was charmed when Philip Slade began inquiring about the Alnaker pictures, promptly made this an excuse to have coffee in the gallery.

If Max had been there, of course, he would undoubtedly have raised an eyebrow. The interest displayed by this new young man seemed to be as much in the insurance and security side as the artistic, to put it mildly. But Max had gone, and Sir John Halford, whose suspicions would indubitably have been aroused, remained at the far end, amiably downing Max's excellent brandy while devoting himself to Lady Inchmory. Julie had returned to the Gate-house, announcing that she was going to bed early, to be ready for the coming week at the Centre.

Veronica herself had no suspicions at all, simply a great thankfulness that through this charming boy she was in touch once again with James.

'I'm so sorry you can't meet James's sister, my daughter, Julie,' she apologized. 'But she had a bad accident last year you know – a fall in a point-to-point, and damaged her spine – and she's still not at all strong, I'm afraid.'

'That's our girl,' Philip told his partner the next day. 'We can't snatch the miniatures. Out of the question. They're much too well guarded. In a special cabinet, all wired up for sound. Security staff thick on the ground, too, with buzzers, intercom, electronic beams. You name it, they've got it, all round their damn gallery. Far too risky to attempt anything there, it would be. But the girl – that's another story. The only daughter, and an invalid. She doesn't even live in the main building, either, but on her own in the Gate-house. No alarm system there. So all we have

184

to do is snatch her, and–'

'And then what, for God's sake?' Ben Morris demanded irritably. Unlike Philip, who came of excellent family – even if they had thrown him out years earlier – and possessed impeccable manners, a vast amount of poise, Ben Morris was not smooth or presentable. Very practical, though, and where Philip had one set of contacts, he had the other. He was much more cautious, too, than Philip, always saw the snags in any plan. 'You must be off your nut,' he said disgustedly. 'We're not kidnappers, for God's sake. Or hijackers. What we are is a small specialist agency, that's what. Dealing in small paintings, china, antique silver and bronzes. You want it, we locate it, obtain it on the quiet, and sell it for the right price. We don't deal in people and we aren't going to start now.'

'I know, but–'

'We're specialists in small valuables, and we're staying that way.'

'Of course we're specialists. Working under contract to obtain specific items. Like these miniatures the Alnakers have. Which, as I've told you, we aren't going to get by ordinary methods. So are we going to back out? Say the job's beyond us? Or do we simply go about it in an entirely different

185

way, for once?'

'Not if it involves snatching a human being, we don't. Apart from anything else, we'd never get away with it.'

'If we plan it carefully enough there's no reason we shouldn't pull it off. And do ourselves a bit of good at the same time, that's what you don't seem to understand. But this job could be a bloody good advertisement for us.'

'Advertising ourselves as thugs and kidnappers won't do us no good. That's quite the wrong image, that is, thanks very much.'

'We shan't advertise ourselves as thugs. We'll go out of our way to be very gentle with the girl. But everyone will see we stop at nothing, once we're contracted to get an item. We don't back out. We show we can handle a big job, and pull it off. The girl's an invalid, it'll be easy, no trouble there. I've thought it right through. Her Dad'll ransom her with the miniatures, a bill of sale to go with them, too, all legal and above-board. The buyer won't even have to hide them away – a bonus for him, that he won't be expecting. Lord Alnaker will know how to keep everything out of the press, too. He's powerful, rich and capable. And he'll be working for us. For his darling daughter's safety.'

'You terrify me, mate, you really do. Suppose he isn't working for us, what then? Suppose he goes to the police, say, or one of the security firms? Or even the security service – he'd know how to go about that, too, wouldn't he? Strewth, we might be dead. And all over a few rotten miniatures that some bloke painted five hundred years ago. It's not worth it.'

'Nothing like that will happen. Lord Alnaker will want his daughter back.'

'You can't be sure. No, I don't like it. Not kidnapping. Suppose we were caught? What sort of sentence would we get? It's not worth it. And how are we supposed to be looking after this damned girl, once we got her? Tell me that.'

Philip knew then that Ben was going to give in. He'd come round to a discussion of ways and means. He might protest still, but he was hooked.

'Nothing can go wrong, if we prepare it carefully enough.'

'Everything can go wrong, if you ask me.'

'Not half as risky as trying to snatch the miniatures, I can tell you that.'

'If the place is swarming with security men, as you say, how are we going to get the girl away? Answer me that.'

'The girl isn't guarded at all. That's the whole point. There she was, on Saturday afternoon sitting in this rose garden in her wheelchair, strumming away on a guitar and singing to herself, with half the population sauntering through the grounds. Anyone who'd cared to cough up the entrance fee.'

'I still don't like it,' Ben said. 'However, I reckon I'd better go down there, nose round myself. You'd better keep out of the place now, they know your face. If I don't like the lie of the land, it's all off. That's final.'

At the Plough in Alnaker St Nicholas, though, Ben found Philip had been right. All he needed to know about Julie Alnaker he learnt in half an hour from old Jim Hodgson, drinking his pint and giving anyone who cared to listen a progress report on old Mrs Hodgson at the Rehabilitation Centre. Mrs Hodgson, the entire public bar explained to the stranger in their midst, went daily to St Mark's in Halchester in an ambulance, which first collected the Hon. Julia Alnaker from the Hall – 'hobnobbing with the lord's daughter now, your missus, Jim, reckons she'll be getting too toffee-nosed for the likes of us' – came on to the post office for Mrs Hodgson, went on to Alnaker Hard for young Barry Fripp, along

188

to Downside to pick up the herdsman's wife at the farm cottages, who had an ankle in plaster after an accident on her moped, and so to the Rehabilitation Centre with its load.

'I must agree, it does look easy enough to get hold of the girl,' Ben admitted.

'I tell you, it's watertight.'

CHAPTER ELEVEN

Toby and Julie

On Wednesday Jo Grant took delivery of the converted Saab, and that evening Julie drove the car round the lanes. On Thursday she told them all about it at the Centre.

'The best thing you can do, Julie, is to drive it in here tomorrow, and we'll give you practice in getting in and out and so on.'

So on Friday the ambulance was cancelled, and Julie – with the assistance of a disapproving Rosie, who wanted to travel in with her – manoeuvred herself into the car, Rosie handed her crutches in after her, and Julie drove triumphantly off alone.

Flushed with success, she rang Toby that evening, told him she was driving herself up to London the following morning.

'Attagirl,' he said cheerfully. 'I've managed to fix a day off, so I'll meet you whenever you like.'

'I should think it would take me about two hours if I come up on the motorway. It always takes Dad an hour and a half, he says, so if I trundle quietly along at my own speed, it still shouldn't take more than two hours. If I leave here at ten, say, I ought to be with you soon after midday.'

'You don't want to drive in over the fly-over. Look, love, I reckon you'd better get off the motorway well before that. I'll meet you outside London somewhere.'

This wasn't at all what Julie had in mind. She wanted to meet Toby in London, have a meal in a coffee bar or some trendy Italian spaghetti house – as unlike the ostentatious Blue Boar as possible – visit his flat, see him at last against the background of the big teaching hospital where he worked, meet some of his friends, in fact, get herself thoroughly orientated as to his life in London. It might not be exactly encouraging, she'd almost certainly run up against some gorgeous nurse who turned out to be his girl friend, have to return home to the Hall in despair. Even so, if she had to find out the worst, she would still be able to imagine Toby in his London hospital and his flat. What good this would do her, she couldn't have explained. But there it was. She was absolutely determined on her course of action. Meet outside London, indeed. Oh, no. Not likely. Not if she knew it. 'I'll be O.K., Toby,' she said airily. 'I'll meet you at the hospital.'

'Oh no you won't, duckie.'

'Why on earth not?'

'Suppose the car broke down? You wouldn't even be able to get out of the car, and—'

'I can get in and out very nicely, thank you, Toby. So there.'

'Oh, I daresay you can, in a nice quiet layby. But not on a motorway. And certainly not on the flyover. No, you can't drive on the flyover, Julie. Have some sense, do. In fact, I'm not tremendously enthusiastic about you driving in central London at all. Not alone, in any case. At least if I was with you, and anything happened, I could pick you up and carry you.' He paused, un-accountably pleased with this notion, and smiled to himself. Carrying Julie would be altogether a very rewarding experience.

Julie thought otherwise. '*Carry* me?' she repeated, in a voice of acute disgust, jolting Toby sharply out of his tender dream. 'Carry me? Toby Grant, I can look after myself thank you very much. You sound exactly like Rosie,' she added, simply to annoy him.

'She's not necessarily always wrong,' he said calmly. 'And I don't think it would be at all wise to–'

'Oh, come off it, Grandpa. If my father and your father see nothing wrong with me driving in the Saab on my own, what possible reason can you find for–'

'Ah, but do they know you're proposing to drive into central London?'

They didn't, of course. And Toby was quite capable of ringing either of them up to check. Then there'd be trouble. 'Well, no,' she had to admit. 'I suppose I haven't actually mentioned exactly what I'm going to do tomorrow. But–'

'We'll meet outside London, love. And that's it.'

'But – look, I've got a radio transmitter. Your father insisted on it. I thought it was a bit silly of him, to tell you the truth. But actually, I must say, now I've got it, it's rather fun. It's a walkie-talkie thing, like the ones the security men carry. I have it with me all the time, and I have to call in when I set off and when I arrive. Acorn 10, that's me,' she added proudly.

Toby sighed long and ostentatiously. 'You'll be out of range after the first five miles, you dopey kid.'

'Oh.'

'Those things aren't magic, sweetie.

They're short-range, for use on the estate. Oh, Dad's quite right, you'd be able to use it to cover your journeys to St Mark's, that would be inside the limits. But a few miles up the motorway, you wouldn't be able to raise a peep from the Hall.'

'But Dad often comes through when he's driving down from London. He's always doing it.'

'Your father has a radio-telephone linked with the G.P.O. Surely you know that? Don't you understand the difference. My God, bird brain, snap out of it.'

'Yes. I see. It didn't occur to me there was any difference, I'm afraid.'

'You haven't actually *got* a radio-telephone in the Saab, have you? They didn't install one when they were doing the conversion, did they?'

'Oh no. No, I haven't anything extra. Only my little transmitter, like the one the men have, with a pop-up aerial, and the battery. I keep it in the glove compartment.'

'You'll be out of touch almost as soon as you're on the motorway,' Toby informed her scathingly. 'Three miles up it, and you'll be on your own. Listen, what we'd better do is meet well outside London. Let's see. Guildford, say. Yes, that'll do us. Very fast trains to

Guildford, too. You go to the station at Guildford as near to midday as you can make it. I'll come down by train about then, and I'll look for the Saab in the station yard. See you then. Guildford station. Midday.' Maddeningly, he put the receiver down.

Julie stared blankly at her own receiver. So much for her dreams. She wasn't going to London at all. 'Guildford,' she said aloud in disgust. 'What on earth is there to do in Guildford, for heaven's sake?'

Frustrated and restless now, she went down in the lift, got into the Saab. She'd go over and see Mrs Hodgson, she decided. That would be something to do, and more useful than sitting about biting her nails in rage and disappointment. She could at least have a good grumble to Mrs Hodgson – these days her chief confidante.

Mrs Hodgson understood at once why Julie was downcast. 'Guildford?' she repeated. 'Well, it's a very nice town, I always think myself, but it isn't what you'd planned exactly is it? You won't be able to see young Toby's flat, after all.'

Julie flushed. She hadn't meant to let on that this formed part of her blue-print for the day. But Mrs Hodgson seldom missed a trick. She had children, grandchildren and great grandchildren, and now, after enduring three generations of teenagers, courting couples and young marrieds, she was about the most with-it great grandma you could lay hands on. Nothing surprised her, she had seen it all before.

'Have you heard from that Rupert?' she asked.

'No. No, I haven't. But he may not have had time. It's only two weeks since I wrote.'

'You wrote airmail, though?'

'Oh yes.'

'He'd have rung up if he was upset.' Mrs Hodgson was sure of this. Any of her grandsons would have been on the telephone inside the hour, she informed Julie, even if they'd had to borrow the money to make the call.

Here, though, for once she slipped up. Her sense of the value of money let her down, was, by Rupert's standards, out of date. What he thought about was not the cost of a telephone call, but of the flight home from Lagos.

Being Rupert, he approached the problem cautiously, took his time. But after some manipulation of appointments in Nigeria, a few half-truths here and there, he had finally persuaded Armitage & Waldron that he needed to return home for consultations in the London office. He had booked his flight at last, would be arriving on Wednesday.

This sort of behaviour, though, was right outside Mrs Hodgson's league. 'If you haven't heard, dearie,' she said stringently, 'I don't think you need bother any more about him.' A mistake as it happened, but neither of them suspected it.

'No, I shan't,' Julie agreed.

'But I'd tell Toby what you've done, if I were you.'

'Yes, I shall.'

'In that case, Julie, you'd better take a picnic with you. Trying to talk across a table in a crowded restaurant on a Saturday, when you've something important you want to say, is very difficult. Might put you off.'

The kitchens at the Hall produced a picnic on a magnificent scale. Two great wicker baskets were filled, and loaded into the Saab. 'If Julie's going out for the day, she can have a proper luncheon basket, none of them Scotch eggs and sausage rolls. She can have the same as what we'd give his Lordship. Why not? She's entitled to it, and she's had a rotten time, poor kid,' the head cook had announced. The rest of the kitchen staff agreed wholeheartedly. While Julie had been shut away in the Gatehouse with Rosie, they'd more or less forgotten her. But now she had taken matters into her own hands again, charging round the corridors in her chair, driving in and out in the Saab, they were united behind her.

So the Glyndebourne baskets were filled with a lavish assortment of food and drink. The tall basket held wine, spirits, beer, mineral waters, ice and an array of glasses, as well as two big flasks of black coffee and one of cream. The square basket was bursting with cold consommé, smoked salmon, cold duck with orange salad, crisp lettuce, strawberry flan, various cheeses, fresh rolls and butter, biscuits, and an assortment of fresh fruit.

Toby nearly fell over, he laughed so much. 'Who did they imagine you were entertaining, love?' he inquired, when at length he could speak. 'Not Jo Grant's boy Toby, that's for sure.'

Julie was pink. 'I don't know what they can have been thinking of,' she said, fussed and embarrassed. 'This is what they give Dad for Glyndebourne or the races. Why on earth they should suppose I–'

'They thought they owed it to your position,' Toby said firmly. About time he remembered it, too, he reminded himself. *'Did* you tell them you were meeting me?' he asked curiously, though he was certain she couldn't have done.

'No. No, I didn't. Because I didn't want them all chewing over my affairs. You see' – she took the plunge – 'I'm not marrying Rupert, and–'

'You're not marrying Rupert? Why not? What's happened?'

Julie's heart plummeted down to her boots. He sounded thoroughly cross about it. She didn't know exactly what she had hoped he'd register at the news, but whatever she had expected, it had not been this cross irritability. 'Well,' she tried to explain, 'you see, I thought–'

'Tell me what's happened, not what you thought,' Toby interrupted her, like an irate consultant on a ward round that was going badly. She had needed him, he saw at once, to play his customary role of elder brother, to mop her up and set her on her feet again. This was what she had wanted to see him about, why she had so startlingly rung him that night. Now she was going to tell him her heart was broken. He was going to spend the day listening to Julie telling him how marvellous Rupert was, how she couldn't bear life without him.

'I wrote to him, you see,' she said in small voice, 'to say I didn't want to marry him. It was finished.' Her voice dwindled miserably into silence.

'To say you didn't want to?' Toby bellowed. Apparently things were not as he'd been imagining at all. He'd got it all wrong. 'Tell me *precisely* what's happened,' he said sternly, sounding like the elder brother he so much didn't want to be. 'First of all, why don't you want to?'

'Because I don't love him,' Julie said in the same small frightened voice.

'Are you sure?'

'Oh, yes. Quite sure.' She nodded. 'I have been for some time,' she added, with more confidence.

Toby at last grasped that she meant what she said, that it was all true. 'Good,' he said briskly. 'I never did think he was the right bloke for you. Nice enough in this way, of course, well meaning and all that. Lightweight, though.'

'L-lightweight?'

'Yeah. You must have noticed, love. Well obviously you did. That's why you found you weren't in love with him, of course.'

'No, it wasn't,' Julie said stubbornly. This

200

at least she knew beyond doubt.

'What was it, then?'

Now or never. Well, it had better be now, however cross he sounded, however much of a fool she made of herself. 'Because I realized I was in love with you,' she said, her voice as cross now as his. She couldn't meet his eyes, stared pugnaciously out across the pale green of the new season's bracken, over the weald spread below the hillside where they'd planned to picnic, watched light and shadow chasing across the fields as high clouds passed over the sun, asked herself what Toby would do now.

After a brief silence, 'You *what?*' he asked flatly.

'Was in love with you, I said.' She shouted it at him, furious he'd made her repeat it.

'You can't be.'

Surprised, Julie brought her eyes back at last from their determined quartering of the countryside, stared at Toby. 'Why not?' she said.

He had closed his eyes, and his face was momentarily unguarded. She could see, quite clearly, why not. Simply that he was afraid to believe her.

So he loved her, then. That was more than she had dared to hope – or was it? A joyous calm certainty settled on her, and she knew that she had dared, had somehow counted on it, had known in her bones that he loved her. She leant forward, kissed him softly on the mouth.

His eyes opened. His arms came round her. They felt like hoops of steel.

This was all she wanted. To be held, by Toby, like this. To the end of her days.

They ate the stupendous meal, drank the wine and the coffee. It was wasted on them. They knew nothing of what they were consuming, had time only for the wonder of each other. Their fingertips touched between each mouthful, their eyes drowned together in blinding radiance. There was so much to talk about, so much to tell. No sentence completed, they interrupted, shouted, bubbled with laughter, shared every thought, every recollection, broke off only to kiss, or trace with wonder the lines of features they had known for ever, that were yet so unbelievably precious.

At last Julie lay back, content simply to let the warm air of midsummer caress her, the cool wind ruffle her hair, the hot sun beat down and warm her to the bones. The heat of the sum lay on the bracken all round them, she could smell its robust scent, tantalizing and pungent. Shutting her eyes, she allowed herself to sink into the quiet hillside. Insects hummed round her, the bracken rustled in the light breeze. She felt she could have remained for ever.

She felt, too, Toby's hand on her wrist, warm and comforting, opened heavy eyelids to find his head close to hers. His own eyes, though, were far away, absent, empty.

Then he released her wrist, his eyes came alive. 'Feeling your pulse,' he told her briefly. 'You're exhausted, aren't you? I'm going to drive you home now.'

'I'm not in the least exhausted.' She sat up. 'You're not going to drive me back. We can–'

'Love,' he said. 'If you could see yourself. Home for you, and an early night. You've done enough for one day.'

But this wasn't at all how she had intended the day to end. 'I'm not going home,' she said obstinately, determined to overcome the lassitude that had taken possession of her. Toby was quite right, of course, she was worn out.

He smiled at her. 'You lie there. I'm going to pack this lot away into the car, in any case. Then we can see.'

So she lay dreamily watching as, neat and

203

methodical, he cleared up the remnants of the vast, meaningless feast, replaced glasses and bottles in their compartments, screwed up paper, collected debris. He wore the same absent, absorbed expression he'd had earlier when he'd been taking her pulse. Then their eyes met, and his long bony face with its touch of melancholy lighted up, and he smiled back at her in a way she'd never known he could smile. A new smile. One for her alone.

He picked up one of the wicker baskets, she heard his footsteps crunching through bracken, downhill to the Saab. Presently they came crunching back, he collected the other basket, strode away again. She lay, listening to his steps receding, let peace spread through her limbs. Overhead, as a lark sang high above, lost in the misty blue of the June sky, the summer day dissolved about her and she drifted into sleep.

She awoke to find Toby kneeling beside her, smiling at her, the new unguarded smile of mutual love. He said, 'Darling Julie,' bent and kissed her, and two bodies melted into one.

Julie could have stayed there for ever, but Toby sat back. 'I'm going to carry you down to the car now,' he told her. He laid a finger against her cheek with tenderness. 'You've flaked right out, love, haven't you?' he said. 'Straight home and then bed for you.'

She looked at him. Allow this joy to escape and be lost? As long as they lived, there would never be another moment like this. 'No,' she said. 'Here in the bracken, like this. Love me.'

His eyes blazed back, but he shook his head.

CHAPTER TWELVE

A Call From Zürich

Max rang Jo Grant from Zürich. 'I've been given some information that seems to present us with a bit of a problem,' he said. 'I thought we'd better have a word.'

Jo sat up. As he knew from many shared experiences, Max was inclined to speak of 'a bit of a problem' when anyone else would have said, 'we're in one hell of a spot'.

'Oh yes,' he said cautiously. 'And what would that be?'

'It appears that fellow at Scotland Yard wasn't so far off the mark, after all. There's word on the grapevine here among the art dealers that our Hilliard miniatures are to be stolen. They think during the next week or two, and they seem confident of the accuracy of their information.'

'In the next week or two?' Jo was startled.

'So they assert. There's a recognized buyer in the market, apparently, who's known to be in touch with a dealer not too fussy about the origin of his stock. He's alleged to be getting hold of them – by some means unknown. And there's our problem.'

'But what does this buyer suppose he's going to do with them, if he gets them? He can't admit possession, can he?'

'Hardly. He'll keep them in his bathroom, I suppose, or in a drawer with his handkerchiefs. Gloat privately. After all, they don't take up any space worth noticing.'

'Seems mad to me,' Jo said sourly.

'Oh, it's mad all right. And if you ask me the whole story is a bit far-fetched. But at least we've had warning. We'll have to take precautions. Will you arrange for additional supervision in the gallery generally, and particular attention to the Hilliards?'

'I'll see to that.'

'You'd better have more men down from London, so that you can increase the security checks and so on. And make sure everyone stays on their toes, won't you?'

'Oh, I'll do that all right,' Jo said, frowning now.

'Well, I leave it to you, Jo. Probably there's nothing in it. Hope not. I'll be back on Wednesday evening, by the way. You might tell them in Park Lane.'

'I'll make a note of that. Is there a plane

you'd like met?'

'Yes. I'll be at Heathrow on the Swissair flight that leaves here at 5 p.m. And I'll want beer and a sandwich in the office, and I'll get down to my papers and the mail. They can leave me an outside line switched through, too.'

'Right. Look, before you go—'

'Yes?'

'About this question of the miniatures. I'd rather handle it from this end entirely, if you don't mind, without having anyone down from London.'

'Whatever you think, Jo, whatever you think. But why not? Can't you do with some extra men?'

Jo grinned to himself. Max had been famous in army days for this little trick. 'Do what you think best, use your own judgement', was frequently followed by 'what the hell do you imagine you're up to? I can't recollect giving authority for... Inform me immediately'.

There had been a technique for dealing with this habit then, and he used it again now, began to answer in elaborate detail. 'Well, you see,' he explained methodically, 'it seems a bit risky to me, you know. After all, down here, I know all the lads, where they live, how they spend their free time, what pubs they use, what girls they're going round with. If they do anything out of the ordinary, it sticks out a mile. But if we have someone down from London, I don't know much about him or his background. Only what I'm told. If he acts out of pattern, I shan't be able to spot it. In fact, they could even slip a man in, and I might be fooled.'

'Right, Jo. Point taken. You do it your way. As long as it's covered.'

'I'll see to that.'

'I'll be down as usual on Friday evening in any case. We can go over the ground in detail then.' He rang off, and Jo had himself put through to the Park Lane office. Not until he had finished talking to them did he remember that he'd told Max nothing about Toby and Julie. He'd promised Toby he'd prepare the ground for him, give Max an inkling of how matters stood, and make an appointment for Toby to go to Park Lane as soon as Max returned. Well, he'd missed the opportunity. The news would have to stand over now until Wednesday. And he couldn't, in view of Max's warning about the Hilliards, afford to leave the Hall, go himself to Heathrow to meet him. He'd have to stay where he was, telephone Max on the

Wednesday evening.

How would Max take the news, he wondered? For once Jo couldn't hazard a guess what his attitude might be. All right, so he was fond of Toby, regarded him as one of the family, had more than once said Jo was lucky, Toby was far easier to get on with than James. But did that mean he'd want to see him marry Julie? Jo couldn't say at all. He didn't even know what he felt about it himself. Toby'd been eating his heart out for Julie for years now, of course. Veronica would fight it hard, though. Awkward, that would be. And the difficulty was there was all that Alnaker money. All right for Max, he was used to it. But could Toby ever come to terms with it, learn how to manage it? He shook his head, then reached for the telephone again. Toby's problems would have to wait.

He rang round the estate, called an emergency meeting of all security staff in the gallery.

Waiting there for them to assemble, he stared dubiously at the Hilliard miniatures in their cabinet, scratched his head in some bewilderment. They were very pretty, of course. No doubt about it. But worth all that amount of money? More than he'd see in a lifetime? It beat him.

Philip Slade was brooding, too, over the value of the Hilliards. He knew precisely what they were worth, of course, and it was a good deal more than he and Ben were getting for their trouble. A pity that, but it couldn't be helped. And even after everyone had been paid off, it would keep them both in what even he considered near-luxury for some years. He couldn't prevent himself wondering, though, if he might not be able to shake Lord Alnaker down for a bit over the odds. The miniatures, plus a bit extra for his daughter's safety? Why not?

On Wednesday morning, he flew in to a small airfield in southern England in a charter plane from France, was met by Ben Morris, driving his elderly and unnoticeable Austin saloon.

Before they left the airfield, though, Philip confirmed the booking he'd made for the following day.

'That's right,' the pilot agreed easily. 'Here at ten-thirty tomorrow for you and your party. I've got it down here.'

'Don't forget I'll have an invalid with me,' Philip nagged. 'And a nurse too. Four of us to travel.'

'All arranged for,' the pilot told him

imperturbably. 'I mentioned it in the office, and they've booked the other plane for you. More room, you see. We often use it for transporting accident cases – especially after skiing holidays.' He grinned. To him it was a huge joke, all these idiots paying good money to break their limbs, be flown home at more expense still. 'Plenty of room for everyone,' he reassured them. 'And I'll be here on time. Not to worry.'

'Good. Because there'll be an ambulance meeting us on the other side, and I've only got it for four hours – they're booked right up, otherwise.'

'I'll be on time,' the pilot promised.

Ben drove to the small hotel in Halchester where he had taken rooms for them both. 'The ambulance is coming down from London at first light tomorrow,' he said. 'And the nurse too.' He opened out his road map. 'They'll pull up at the snack place on the motorway, here, for breakfast, stay there until we meet them. We should have time to drive over the route and you can do your telephoning from the box there, too.'

'Sounds all right.' Philip yawned. 'Let's break for a cup of tea. Afterwards we can look at the French maps, and I'll bring you up to date on the arrangements there.'

At five o'clock the same afternoon, Julie left Mrs Hodgson at the sweetshop, drove on through the village, turned into the park.

Drawing up at the Gatehouse, she swung round, reached for the elbow crutches. As she was levering herself up into a standing position, a yellow Mini drew up on the gravel alongside the Saab. Dick Watson, one of Jo's security staff.

'Hope I haven't kept you waiting, Miss Alnaker,' he said.

'No, I've only just arrived,' Julie reassured him. 'Good timing, in fact. Thanks for answering my call.'

'And what have you got now?' He came over to join her. 'New equipment, is it?'

'A ChairMobile. The Centre have lent it to me to try out at home, but I'm not up to getting it out of the car and upstairs myself. That's why I called.'

'Fine. I'll do that for you.' He opened the back of the Saab, looked in. 'This is a Chair-Mobile, is it?'

'Invented by Lord Snowdon – for people like me, they say at the Centre. The seat swivels, and the height is adjustable. You can still drive round on it. It's really a mobile platform.'

'With a steering column. Splendid little job, it looks.'

They went up in the lift together, and then Julie sat on the ChairMobile. 'Slightly high for me,' she said, 'but I think I'll keep it like this for a bit.'

'I could bring it down for you if you like,' Dick Watson suggested – longing, in fact, to get his hands on the works.

'I think it may be quite useful at it is,' Julie said, moving backwards and forwards experimentally.

'Just as you feel,' Dick agreed, disappointed. 'No trouble, though,' he added hopefully.

Julie shook her head. 'Not just yet, anyway. Thanks all the same.' She drove through to the kitchen, began to practise lifting saucepans, the electric kettle, opening cupboards, turning on taps. 'Good reach, you see,' she pointed out. 'That's why they've got it high, of course. I'll keep it like this, I think.' She put the saucepans back, opened and shut the fridge, then the oven. 'Great,' she said. 'This is worthwhile. I'm going to have one of these of my own.'

'Certainly seems useful,' Dick agreed, 'efficient, too. And smart, I reckon. Straight out of some very streamlined science project. Tomorrow's world.'

Julie was delighted, and after he'd left she went through into the hall, surveyed herself in the big mirror there. He had been right, she decided. The ChairMobile itself gave a general impression of brisk efficiency, made her look like a scientific assistant from a shiny laboratory, using the latest mechanized equipment available in her job. No longer like a pale invalid in a secluded backwater, sheltered and cosseted.

Enthusiastically ready to demonstrate the ChairMobile to whoever should appear, she was pleased to hear the lift coming up again.

The doors slid open, revealed Veronica. In a flaming temper, was immediately clear.

Too angry even to see the ChairMobile, she stopped where she was, in front of the lift. 'So there you are,' she said. 'I've just had a telephone call from Rupert.' The announcement was unmistakably a challenge.

Julie looked back at her set lips. She was beginning to be furious herself. Bloody Rupert. What did he mean by saying nothing to her, getting on to Veronica instead?

'I was *astonished* at what he had to tell me,' Veronica continued.

Julie stared back at her. When Veronica had first stepped out of the lift, obviously in a rage

215

of some sort, Julie had been momentarily unnerved. But now she was simply angry. What
business had her mother and Rupert to discuss her in this way? It was coming to something if she was to be ticked off like a
disobedient ten-year-old for breaking her
own engagement. In fact, it was ridiculous.
She caught sight of herself in the mirror
again, and this gave her renewed confidence.

'I've broken my engagement,' she said
clearly. 'If Rupert has anything to say about
it, he can say it to me himself.'

'I told him not to,' Veronica said shortly.

'Why? What's it got to do with you?'

Two pairs of eyes crossed.

'I won't be treated like this,' Veronica said.

Julie had a sudden, wholly unexpected,
and somewhat frivolous impulse to say 'You
will, you know'. She swallowed it, said only,
'But really, Mother, I should have thought it
was entirely between Rupert and me.'

'Do you think I'm going to stand by and
do nothing, watch you throw your future
away for some whim?'

'It's not a whim.'

'What is it then?'

'I've thought about it a lot.'

'You've said nothing to me. Or to Rosie.'

'Why should I? I've thought about it, and

216

I've found I don't love Rupert, I don't want to spend my life with him.'

Veronica snorted. 'Love,' she said. 'Grow up. What do you suppose that's got to do with it?'

'Everything.'

'You're simply showing me exactly what I suspected all along. You're young and silly. You don't know what you're talking about. Can't you see when you're well off? Don't you realize you've been extraordinarily lucky that Rupert has stuck by you all this time? More than many men would have done.'

'I know.'

'And now, simply because you've decided you aren't head over heels in love, you calmly break it off. Without even telling me.'

This final sentence was unwise. Julie replied to it with aplomb. 'You must agree, Mother,' she said, 'that Rupert had every right to be the first to hear from me. I was waiting for his answer before I said anything to anyone else. He seems to have got straight on to you instead of me. I must say I don't quite understand why.'

Veronica heard her out with mounting irritation. 'You sound exactly like your father,' she complained.

Julie could tell this was true. What was more, she realized, she probably felt like him, too. For her reaction, much as his would have been, was a recognition that Veronica was obviously intent on making a scene, and had to be handled, but that the uproar had little to do with the real point at issue.

'Look, Mother,' she began again, as reasonably as she knew how. 'I don't want to marry Rupert. Nothing is going to change that. It's between me and him, and if he wants to talk about it, of course I'll explain exactly why. I know I've changed my mind, I know it's unfair to him when he's been so terribly kind all the time I've been ill. I appreciate it, and I've told him so. I'll tell him again. But what I won't do is marry him.'

'If I have anything to do with it you will,' Veronica said crisply.

Julie's patience evaporated. 'But you don't have anything to do with it,' she retorted. 'It's a decision for me. No one else. I am not going to marry Rupert. That's final.'

'There's nothing final about it. You'll do as I say.'

They might have been back in the nursery, Julie saw. The situation was laughable, except that neither of them was in any mood for humour. 'Where is Rupert, anyway?' she asked. Was he in Nigeria? Or London? Or downstairs, perhaps, lurking by the lift until Veronica told him to appear?

'In London,' her mother said repressively. 'He flew back especially to see you. But I told him I'd deal with all this nonsense.'

Julie sighed, looked a little helplessly at Veronica. Back to square one. She appeared honestly to believe that none of this was more than a lot of nonsense, and thought herself more than capable of sorting out two silly children, who had begun quarrelling over nothing. 'Mother, I'm not a child. I'm going to choose my own husband, and it won't be Rupert. I've told him so, and both he and you really must accept it.'

'Oh indeed, and who do you imagine you are going to marry, pray?' Veronica was scathing.

Julie couldn't resist it. 'Toby,' she said.

That did it.

What remained of Veronica's self-control and common-sense finally snapped. Her remarks about the Grant family, father and son, were outright melodrama, so lurid that Julie didn't even start to take them seriously.

'Don't be gothic, Mother. The fact that I'm going to marry Toby isn't any sort of conspiracy directed at you. In fact, it's nothing to do with you.'

'Jo Grant has always hated me,' Veronica stated, not for the first time. 'This is aimed at *me*, don't you understand?'

'No. I think,' Julie said with a lack of inhibition that startled her, 'that for once you must relinquish the centre of the stage. This concerns me, and not you at all.' It seemed so obvious that it almost spoke itself. Even so, she'd never spoken to Veronica in this way before, and she was shaken.

Not as shaken as Veronica, though. Defeat stared her in the face, and she knew it. However, she made a convincing attempt to disguise her rout. 'I shall go straight up to Park Lane to see your father, tell him what you propose to do,' she said with dignity. 'If you won't listen to me perhaps you'll pay attention to him.' She went to the telephone. 'I want the Rolls at the front entrance in half an hour,' she said, replaced the instrument, and returned to the lift. She pressed the button, the doors opened, she stepped inside, they closed.

She had gone.

Julie discovered that she was both elated and extremely hungry. In her turn, she raised the telephone, asked the switchboard to put her through to her father as soon as he could be reached. This settled, she drove the ChairMobile smartly back into the kitchen. The day had come to cook for herself.

Years ago, over a primus stove up on the moors, the Grants had taught her to cook eggs and bacon. Sausages, too. Since then, she had learned to produce a passable omelette, some good salads. If put to it, she could grill chops or steaks, deal with a few frozen vegetables. No more. No casseroles, no pastry, no puddings, no roasts even, though Mrs Hodgson assured her that a roast was the easiest dish in the world. Somewhere she'd have to learn some elementary cooking, and fast, for she and Toby had always shared a longing for a small personal home of their own. No staff, no institutional amenities. Neither of them had in practice ever lived anything but what amounted to institutional life – you could call it a hotel, she admitted, rather than a hostel. It had never been a home.

Now Julie broke eggs into the frying pan, hungrily added bread too, and bacon and tomatoes, plugged in the coffee percolator, heated milk. A hard day at the Centre had made her ravenous. Happiness, too, improved her appetite. And confidence.

For now she had confidence in her ability to deal, not only with Veronica, but with the future, whatever it proved to be. Confidence that one day she'd regain her health. She had a long way to go before she recovered the full use of her legs, but she was sure that in the end she'd achieve this. Walking might never again become the easy, thoughtless activity it had once been, and she couldn't imagine that she'd be able to run freely across the moorland turf. Toby thought she'd be able to ride, though, that soon she'd explore the woods and moors on horseback again. Not on Rufus, of course. On some quiet, steady, reliable pony instead. But outdoor hours in the saddle, picnics and the wind in her hair – all this would be hers again, Toby swore. And that she'd make her own way in life, upright and on her two feet, she no longer had any doubt. After all, from the elbow crutches she was using now they'd promised that next week she'd progress to two sticks. Soon it would be one only. At last, she hoped, none. Walking unaided. Together, she and Toby could achieve anything. She toasted them both in a mug of coffee. The future was golden.

CHAPTER THIRTEEN

Park Lane

The switchboard girl at the Hall failed to see her own future bathed in any sort of golden glow.

'But I can't tell her *that,* Mr Grant,' she protested. 'She'll be livid. Whatever could I say, anyway? "I'm sorry, the Rolls isn't available, your ladyship, will you have the Jaguar instead, and exactly how long do you want it for?" You know what she's like when she's on the warpath. She'd tell me straight off I could have my cards, I shouldn't wonder. And I like working here.'

'All right, I'll tell her myself,' Jo said wearily. 'You'd better put me through.'

'Oh, *thank* you, Mr Grant. I warn you, she's in a foul mood. Oh, and you did say the Rolls had gone to Heathrow, didn't you? Because Miss Alnaker wants to speak to his lordship.'

'He should be off the plane in about half an hour, if the flight's on time.' So Veronica was in a foul mood, and Julie ringing her father urgently. Jo could read the tea leaves as well as anyone, and it looked to him as if the news had broken. Not the ideal moment for him to choose to have a battle with Veronica over the car service.

It wasn't.

His opening, of course, as the switchboard had foreseen, was bound to be inauspicious. 'I believe you wanted the Rolls, Lady Alnaker.' It had been Max and Jo for over twenty years, but never anything less formal than Lady Alnaker and Mr Grant. Even then, Jo was pretty sure Veronica would have preferred 'my lady' and 'Grant'. 'I'm afraid it isn't available. Would you like–'

'Why isn't it available?' Veronica was indignant. Odious man, how dared he take it on himself to refuse her the car when she ordered it?

'It's at Heathrow, meeting Lord Alnaker. And he's taking it back to Park Lane. So, as I say, I was wondering if you'd like the Jaguar? If so–'

'I shall have to like it, shan't I?' Veronica said tartly, the ground having been cut neatly from under her feet. 'If the Rolls isn't here, obviously I can't have it. I wish you'd said so in the first place.'

224

Jo prayed for patience – a not uncommon reaction when dealing with Veronica in one of her tempers. 'Shall you be driving yourself, Lady Alnaker?' he inquired.

'Driving *myself?*' Though this was what she normally preferred, Veronica succeeded in sounding scandalized. 'All the way to London?' She made it sound more like 'All the way overland to Baghdad'. 'Certainly not.' Just let him *dare* to make difficulties about a driver.

'You're going to London, then?' Jo said. This was the information he'd been after, and he was thankful to have obtained it so easily. 'Then you'll want a driver who can stay up overnight, I expect.'

'Naturally.'

Just over two hours later, Veronica arrived in Park Lane. Max was consuming smoked-salmon sandwiches and Guinness, dictating into his machine, and throwing pieces of paper and succinct instructions at his personal assistant.

Veronica, who had had a chance to think matters over on the journey up – sitting rather grandly alone in the back of the Jaguar – recognized she was on distinctly shaky ground. Max had never wanted Julie to marry Rupert, he'd simply put up with the unavoidable. So she couldn't honestly expect any support from him. He'd be on Julie's side.

She was right. What was more, Julie had already reached him on the telephone, he'd had a talk to Jo, even spoken briefly to Toby at the Central London Hospital. 'The boy's tied up this evening,' he told her. 'But he's coming round to breakfast tomorrow morning. Good, isn't it? Must say I'm delighted.' This was devilish of him, as he didn't need telling – though he had been told, in detail – how very far from delighted his wife would be. 'I was relieved to hear it was all over with Rupert,' he added.

Veronica opened her mouth to say she wasn't, at the last moment substituted the milder statement that she'd been astonished to learn the engagement had been broken off.

Max chuckled. 'Neither of them thought fit to inform us of the state of play, I agree.' He shrugged. 'Young people, my dear.'

Max's personal assistant, quite sure that none of this was meant for her, assembled the pieces of paper that had been flying around, slipped unostentatiously from the room. Max's eyes followed her. 'Good,' he said. 'Now we can be plain. Frankly, Nicky,

I'm thankful not to have that lad for my son-in-law, even more thankful to learn Julie's not in love with him. There may or may not have been anything in all that gossip about him and that girl of yours – Samantha, was it?'

Veronica drew in her breath sharply. In all the excitement she'd managed to forget about Samantha and the part she'd played. 'But–' she began.

'I hoped when we got him off to Nigeria that the engagement might come to a natural end. As it has done. After all, a man who is talked about with another girl during his engagement doesn't exactly fill me with confidence as to my daughter's future happiness.' He glared across his desk, and barked, in a manner familiar in the City – and far from unknown to his wife – 'would you say?'

Veronica unwillingly supposed not. 'But–'

'And Julie and Toby seem to have fixed things up between them. Now that's something I've always hoped for.' He beamed.

This was going too far. 'Toby Grant?' Veronica exploded. 'You never breathed a word about it, Max, I must say, I had no idea–'

'Hardly dared so much as think it,' he admitted with a rueful smile. 'Thought it was too much to hope for, you know.'

Veronica held her breath, did her best to count ten, and considered the situation. Useless to complain to Max about Jo Grant, she knew. She'd tried it often enough in the early days of their marriage, and it never worked. But Toby was simply a lout.

'Toby is simply a lout,' she observed distastefully.

'All young men are louts,' Max agreed. 'But Toby's rapidly outgrowing that stage, I'm pleased to notice.'

'You don't suppose,' Veronica began doubtfully – it wasn't going to be the least use saying this, she could tell, but all the same she was going to have it out – 'You don't suppose he's after her money?'

'Rupert, yes. Not Toby, though. No. Fall over backwards to avoid it, if I know him. And of course I do know him.'

This was more or less what he had told Jo, when he had come on the telephone earlier. 'Splendid, Jo, aren't you delighted?' he'd bellowed down the line. 'She's got rid of that drip Rupert at last, and she and Toby have fixed matters up, she tells me. Best news for a long while, eh?'

'I'm not sure it's right,' Jo was not ready to share these transports.

'Not right? In what way not right?'

'Toby's my son, and he's a good lad, but–'

'Of course he is. None better.'

'But–'

'But what, then?'

'What I said. I'm not sure it's right. In other circumstances, it might–'

'What do you mean, other circumstances? There are no other circumstances.'

'There's the money, as well as the rank,' Jo said unhappily.

Max had demolished these thoughts. 'I'm not having those two kept apart because of some old-fashioned notions of Jo's about money and rank,' he told Veronica. 'It didn't,' he remarked, in one of his rare moments of aristocratic absence of any sort of tact, 'bother me when I was thinking of marrying and I see no reason why thoughts like that should be allowed to come between Julie and Toby. Do you?' He produced his alarming bark for the second time that evening, and Veronica felt compelled to become his dutiful echo and say no, she didn't. 'After all,' Max went on, a little nostalgically, 'I can remember the Hall – and this house, too – when I was a boy and my grandmother was running things. Very different from now. Though that was in the thirties, and even then all the talk was of how society had deteriorated since the great days of the Edwardian era. Well, you and I have seen another series of changes since then, and we've kept the place going, after a fashion. Though this house, where there used to be great balls with royalty present, is simply an office with a *pied-à-terre* for us in the attics. The managing director and his wife, that's all we are.' He said this often enough. Veronica had never cared for it, and she didn't now. 'What will have happened by the time Julie and Toby's children grow up?' Max demanded, answered himself with a shrug. 'No idea. But so long as they've a roof over their heads, three square meals a day, that's good enough for me. And you can rely on Toby to provide that.'

Veronica sighed. She wanted a good deal more than three square meals a day, of course, but that she was wasting her time in opposition was clear. Max and Julie together would win through. She'd better give in, sooner rather than later, plan another wedding. Not the one she'd hoped for. And somehow she'd have to get used to Jo Grant. That would take some doing. 'Where,' she asked reluctantly, 'do you suppose they'll want to be married?'

Max's eyes danced. Victory.

'Can't imagine.' He shrugged again. 'You'd better find out. Lay it on, eh? If you think Rosie isn't up to it, you could always have that girl Samantha back.'

Veronica brightened. 'I wonder if I could? That's quite an idea. Just for the wedding, you know. I wouldn't want her all the time.'

'I could ring up the agency and see if she's free.'

'I must make some lists,' Veronica said, pleased. Then her eyes widened in horror. 'Oh, my God,' she said blankly. 'Rupert. He's supposed to be coming down tomorrow. To lunch. Whatever can I say?' She pulled a face, compounded of guilt, a somewhat shame-faced appeal, and gaiety. It had enchanted millions in her day, could still enchant her husband, even after thirty years of not altogether ideal marriage.

'Want me to rescue you, Nicky?' he inquired tolerantly. 'I'll talk to him, if it would help.'

'Oh Max darling, how angelic. It would relieve my mind.'

'Give me the number, then, and I'll deal with him.'

Max was alone when he greeted Toby over the breakfast table the next morning. Veronica had worked late on her lists, was still sleeping.

The small dining room – once a servant's bedroom, now part of the penthouse flat, its sliding windows opening on to a balcony overlooking Hyde Park – smelt cheerfully of coffee and bacon. Max in a dark London suit was formal in appearance, but ebullient, with a vast immovable grin.

Toby was formal too. In the dark suit he donned for examinations and interviews, and a Central tie, he towered over his future father-in-law. Exuded, though, the same aura of irrepressible joy.

'I hope,' he began diffidently enough, 'you don't mind–'

'Mind? I've always felt you were part of the family, Toby. But now you'll be joining us officially, so to speak. Relieves my mind enormously that Julie – ah well, never mind. Forget it. What concerns us now is the future.' Like the banker he was, he became exact about trusts, investments, income, covenants. Toby for once began to panic, had to be reassured.

Towards the end of the meal, the telephone shrilled.

Max frowned. 'I told them we weren't to be disturbed,' he said, puzzled more than anything else.

The telephone shrilled again.

Max put down his coffee cup. 'What can they be thinking of?' he asked mildly.

The telephone shrilled again, imperiously.

'Oh dear,' Max said. 'Evidently they do really mean it.' He put his hand out, picked the instrument up. 'Yes?' he said curtly.

The telephone was vehement. Max went still. *'What?'* he said.

The telephone gabbled excitedly.

'Where?' he asked, in a tone Toby never remembered hearing from him, though Jo would have known it.

The telephone talked on.

'Very well,' he said. 'I'll come down immediately. Keep in touch.' He replaced the telephone, stood up.

'That was the Hall,' he said heavily. 'They seem to think some thugs have kidnapped Julie.'

CHAPTER FOURTEEN

Hold-Up

Early on the same morning Rupert woke, saw himself in no flattering light. Since he landed at Heathrow, he knew, he'd made nothing but mistakes, had allowed himself to be bullied first by Veronica, then by Max. Resolutely, he showered and dressed. Today would be different. He'd drive down to the Hall, arrive as early as he decently could, have it out with Julie. This was what he should have done in the first place, he saw. Why had he permitted Veronica to act as go-between?

As he drove out of London over the Hammersmith flyover, the air was fresh, held all the promise of a summer morning. He caught a glimpse of the river, glittering in the sun, while above him the sky was blue, small white clouds scudding across in the fresh breeze.

The same breeze blew dust, torn pieces of old newspaper and empty coke cans round

234

the motorway service station outside Halchester. Philip Slade and Ben Morris were breakfasting with the ambulance driver and the nurse.

Their plan, though it had little else to recommend it, had at least the merit of simplicity. They intended to cancel the ambulance from St Mark's, use their own vehicle to collect Julie. They would drug her, drive her to the airfield, fly her out of the country. After this they would open negotiations with her parents. At this stage, of course, their scheme might well have collapsed in any case, none of them being anywhere near a match for Max Alnaker. However, it ran into trouble long before this, right at the outset, in fact. At eight o'clock Philip left his companions drinking a final cup of tea, went to telephone the hospital.

At eight fifteen he was back in the motorway snack bar. 'Outside,' he said briefly.

A glance at his expression and they followed him immediately.

'What's up?' Ben asked.

'The damned ambulance doesn't call for her any more. It's all been changed.' He was furious. 'I told you, Ben, one of us ought to stay down here, keep an eye on the place. But you wouldn't have it, were all for us staying out of sight until we were ready for action. Now you see what it's led to. The bloody girl drives herself now. And picks up someone in Alnaker St Nicholas on the way.'

'Hell.'

'How can she drive herself? I thought you said she was a wheelchair case?' the nurse protested.

'So she was.'

'What are we going to do now?' the driver demanded.

'We'll have to pack it in,' Ben said. 'No option.'

This thoroughly sound advice appealed to no one.

'Do you mean I've driven all the way down here for nothing?' The ambulance driver was disgusted.

Philip and Ben exchanged a long look, the same thought in both their minds. He would have to be paid.

The nurse was annoyed too. 'I've told my agency I won't be available for several weeks,' she said, 'I thought you said it was all fixed.'

'Then you'll have to tell them different, won't you?' Ben retorted sharply, alarmed at the prospect of being expected to pay her for weeks on end.

Both driver and nurse began to complain in unison.

Philip took a hand. 'Let's keep our cool,' he suggested smoothly. 'Of course you'll be paid, if we have to call it off. But do we have to? We've nearly an hour to spare still. Let's try using our heads, shall we?'

'There's that plane coming over, too,' Ben added. More cash to be paid out, he meant, none coming in.

'All that's changed is that we can't have the ambulance drive up to the Hall and collect the girl, no questions asked. But she's still going to leave there, drive to this Centre. Can't we pick her up somewhere between the two?'

Ben took his map out, spread it over the bonnet of the Austin.

Cupidity won the day. Greed make them blind to the risks of the hazardous stop-gap plan they evolved between them. They piled into Ben's old car, drove round the lanes to check the new arrangements, returned to the motorway service area to collect the ambulance. The scheme was on.

'I don't like it,' the nurse protested, not for the first time. 'Not with this old lady in the car. I don't want two of them on my hands. I was told only one patient.'

'You won't have her on your hands, Marj,' Ben assured her. 'I keep telling you, she won't be no trouble. She's the old lady they were talking about that evening I spent in the pub down here. She's had a stroke. We can leave her sitting in the car – you needn't be lumbered with her at all.'

'That's right. Nothing she can do – she'll have to stay there until someone comes along the lane.' Philip backed Ben up, turned to the driver. 'And as far as you're concerned, it's a pushover. You don't have to do anything. Ben and I will get the girl out of the car. All you need do is block the lane at that bend, and then when we're ready, drive to the airfield.'

The driver shrugged, lit a cigarette. 'O.K.,' he said. 'Up to you.'

Philip looked at his watch. 'We'd better be moving off. Go to the bend in the lane and wait. Until we arrive, you're having a quiet smoke before collecting a private patient, if anyone happens along. Be seeing you.'

Although the new plan hardly deserved to succeed, it went like clockwork. Drawn up in the Austin by the park gates, ostensibly studying the map, Philip and Ben watched Julie turn out in the Saab, move down the village street, pull up outside the sweetshop.

'Told you so,' Ben said.

'And here comes the old lady,' Philip added. 'Doesn't look as if we'd have much difficulty with her, does it?'

That, of course, was their mistake. An understandable one, however, for old Mrs Hodgson, looking every one of her eighty-three years, came slowly down the brick path supported by two crutches and with her husband on one side and her daughter-in-law on the other to provide additional assistance. Obviously she was not going to be capable of getting out of the car in a hurry, if at all, the watchers in the Austin were pleased to see. It took two assistants and nearly five minutes to put her into it.

'Good thing we didn't call it off,' Ben said. 'Inside the hour we should be out at the airfield and away.'

He followed the Saab down the main street of Alnaker St Nicholas, into the narrow lane. Half-way along, at the bend as they had planned, the ambulance was pulled out across the full width.

Julie opened her door, leaned out interrogatively, saw that the car behind her had drawn up too. Its driver, she decided, had better legs than she had, could make inquiries for both of them.

He came along, bent down to speak to her.

'Can you see what's happened?' Julie asked. 'Has there been an accident?'

Suddenly he had a gun in his hand. 'Just keep still,' he told her. 'Then no one will be in any trouble. Understand?'

'But what—'

A nurse in uniform appeared from the ambulance. 'We're going to move you into the ambulance, dear,' she said. 'Just relax and you'll be quite comfortable.'

Ben brought the gun nearer. 'Co-operate,' he said. 'I don't want to have to injure the old lady, do I?' Philip appeared behind him, he and the nurse lifted Julie out of the Saab, across to the ambulance, waiting with its doors wide, dumped her unceremoniously on one of the blanket-covered bunks.

Ben followed them, his gun steady.

'Now, dear,' the nurse began in a routine way, getting on with her job as a good nurse should. But for the gun they might have been in outpatients, Julie thought irritably. 'I'm just going to give you this small injection. It won't hurt, and it's not dangerous at all, so you needn't worry. Simply a tiny prick, that's all. So would you take off your coat, dear, and roll up your sleeve for me?

240

That's right.'

Taking off her coat, rolling up her sleeve, Julie watched the man with the gun. He, naturally, had his eyes on her. The ambulance driver, in his seat still, was talking to Philip.

None of them were watching old Mrs Hodgson, none of them saw her reach into the glove compartment, take the little two-way radio in her hand, extend the aerial as she'd seen Julie do. 'Oh dear,' she was muttering to herself, 'I do hope I'm going to be able to do this properly. You press this button here at the side, and announce yourself.' She was much too worried about the importance of carrying out this technique correctly to bother about details like men in the lane pointing guns at people, though she kept her head and hands low, beneath the shield of the instrument panel. She began to transmit – or at least she fervently hoped that was what she was doing. 'Acorn Ten,' she announced in her clear elderly voice. She had often heard Julie begin like this. 'Acorn Ten,' she repeated, quavering.

Meanwhile, down the lane from the Halchester end, rocketing along hell for leather, because the traffic had been bad and he was afraid he might be going to miss Julie, came Rupert.

241

Seeing the ambulance drawn up across the bend, he brought the white M.G.B. to a halt with a scream of brakes, stuck his head out of the window, asked what was going on.

The man talking to the ambulance driver said something he couldn't catch, and Rupert glanced behind him to see if the road was clear for him to back. When he looked forward again he found himself staring into the muzzle of an automatic pistol.

'Stay where you are,' Philip said. 'Don't move.'

'What on earth–?'

Rupert, Julie saw with a sigh of relief. Dark and handsome as ever, appearing from nowhere at the crucial moment, like a knight in an old story, to rescue her.

But this wasn't an old story, and the other man had a gun. Oh, she prayed, be careful, Rupert, be careful.

Even the nurse had suspended her preparations for giving the injection, was watching through the ambulance window with Julie.

Philip called out to her.

'Yes?'

'Have you got that syringe ready?'

'Yes,' she said guiltily. 'It's all ready. I'm just going to–'

'Leave the girl with Ben, then, and bring it

here. You've got plenty of the stuff with you, haven't you?'

'Oh yes. Ben said to—'

'Then come and use it on this bloke. The girl can have hers while we're on the way. We need to put this one out first.'

The nurse jumped down into the lane, walked round the ambulance towards Rupert. Ben stayed where he was, his gun steadily on Julie.

'Out of the car,' Philip told Rupert. 'Stand up.'

'Take your jacket off,' the nurse added, going into her routine again. 'Roll up your sleeve, will you?'

In a minute, Julie thought, she's going to say 'Just a little prick, and it won't hurt'.

Rupert took off his jacket, stood there in the lane, rolling up his sleeve.

'And get into the back of the car now,' Philip said. 'Hand the nurse that rug on the back seat first, though.'

Rupert leant in, took out the rug, gave it to the nurse.

'What am I supposed to do with this?' she asked Philip indignantly.

'Just leave it anywhere for a minute,' he said impatiently, afraid – correctly, as it happened – that time and luck were running out on them. 'Hurry up,' he said to Rupert. 'Get into the back seat. That's right. Now give it to him, then, Marj.'

Ten seconds later Rupert went out like a light.

So much for Rupert, Julie thought, her knight in shining armour. Guns turned out to be more powerful than any number of good intentions. Now she could only hope that the injection, whatever it had been, would do him no real harm.

'Throw the rug over him,' Philip said to the nurse. She did this, he slammed the door of the M.G.B., came round to the back of the ambulance again. 'O.K., Marj, you get on in and prepare another dose for the girl,' he said. 'Bloody nuisance that was,' he added to Ben. 'But the bloke's out for the count now. He'll be no trouble.'

'Right. We'd better get off. We've been hanging around for too long as it is. I'll go with Marj and the girl. You follow in the Austin.'

But they were already too late. Rupert had gained the few minutes of extra time that were needed, and now, bucketing along the narrow lane from the village came the Land-Rover from Alnaker Hall, flat out, and screamed to a halt. Half the security staff from the Hall spilled out.

Philip hadn't a chance. Half in and half out of the Austin's driving seat, he was only beginning to reach for his gun when two of them landed on him.

Behind the Land-Rover the tyres of the little yellow Mini screeched as it braked hard, men stormed out.

But Ben had his gun, and was ready for them. His back against the ambulance, he said, 'One step more, any of you, and I fire.'

In front of the security men was Jo Grant.

No gun was going to stop him, Julie knew. Only a bullet would stop Jo. Out in front and coming fast, he'd hurl himself bodily at Ben's gun. The men from the Hall would follow him. They'd win through, there were so many of them. She was safe now.

But unless she did something about it, Jo was very likely going to be killed.

Ben repeated his order. 'Stop now or I fire.'

Jo was still ten yards away. And he wasn't stopping.

There was only one thing to do, and Julie did it. Pushing off with her hands, she threw herself down on top of Ben, just as the gun went off.

EPILOGUE

Max was anything but congratulatory. 'You both of you took outrageous risks,' he told them curtly. 'Neither of you is to attempt anything of the sort again.'

'I hope not, Dad, certainly,' Julie said, chuckled. 'I don't plan to spend my spare time throwing myself on top of men with guns in country lanes, I promise you.'

'All I've ever looked for is a quiet life in the country,' Jo announced plaintively. 'But perhaps Julie should learn ju-jitsu. Or karate, perhaps. She might have quite an aptitude.' He nodded. 'Same as you had, of course,' he said to Max. 'Like father, like daughter.' He surveyed his employer reminiscently.

'For Pete's sake, don't encourage the girl,' Toby protested. 'She's going to stay quietly at home, learning cooking, not karate.'

'At any rate,' Max reinforced this view, 'the immediate programme is undoubtedly to stay quietly at home.'

'You'll have to have some X-rays, too,' Toby added. 'I don't think you've done

246

yourself any damage, apart from bruising and those grazes I've seen to, but we'll have to be on the safe side.'

By lunch time Dr Buckland had been, an X-ray appointment had been made at St Mark's, while Toby had been on to the Central, had spoken to his stand-in, had promised to catch the next train back to London.

'I think you may possibly be justified in leaving matters here in my hands now,' Max told him with a gleam of distinctly sardonic humour, as they drove to the station. 'Come down as soon as you can, won't you? This week-end?'

'I shall move heaven and earth. That's why I'm going back now.'

'By Saturday we should know how Julie is, if she's done herself any further damage by jumping that maniac and his gun.' He was already beginning to be proud of his daughter. 'I'll take her into St Mark's myself this afternoon. I can look in and see how Rupert is at the same time. You think he'll be all right, you say, once he's come round from that rather powerful dose?'

'It seems to have been simply a quick-acting general anaesthetic, by all accounts. As soon as it's worn off, he'll be back to normal, I should say.'

Max dropped Toby just in time to catch the London train, and drove to the police station. Here he had a talk to the superintendent, and picked out a photograph of Philip Slade, who had already been recognized by two of the security men. They had noticed him when he had had dinner at the Hall, been shown round the gallery by Veronica. The next hurdle was to get over to her the danger she had landed them in by taking this young man at his face value, accepting him so wholeheartedly, merely because he claimed acquaintance with James.

Veronica at once blamed herself for gullibility – not a characteristic she cared to display. It was a harder blow, though, for her to face the knowledge that James had sent no messages, had never tried to be in touch with her. However, in a day or two she was absorbed in planning the wedding, making Rosie sort through the files that Samantha had opened. As far as anyone could tell, the original arrangements were going to be reintroduced as they stood.

'At least,' she said happily to Rosie, 'Julie will be able to wear that lovely dress of Mark Midwinter's after all.'

Over this, though, and many other plans

dear to her heart, she was doomed to disappointment. Neither Julie nor Toby showed any inclination to fit in with her proposals.

Toby's main aim was to persuade Julie to stop attending the Rehabilitation Centre in Halchester, go to the Central London Hospital instead for physiotherapy. He thought she should be admitted to the private wing there. 'Apart from anything else,' he told her, 'it would be a great relief to me. I find it very difficult to concentrate on surgery when I'm constantly imagining you being held up at gun point in Plough Lane. If only you were in London with me, I could keep my eye on you.'

'Well, of course,' Julie said agreeably – and somewhat to his surprise – 'I'd much rather be in London with you, too.'

'That's settled, then.' Toby clinched it while he had the chance. 'In any case, I think it would do no harm for you to be thoroughly reassessed.' He explained the sort of thing he had in mind.

Julie agreed affably. 'Sounds as if it might be quite a long job, though,' she said. 'So we'd better get married, almost at once, hadn't we? Then when I leave the private wing, I can simply come and live with you in your Central flat, can't I? While I go on with my treatment.'

'And cook my supper, too.' Toby was taken with this. 'That's a great idea. I'm all for it.'

'I daresay you'll hardly ever be there to eat it. Stuck in the theatre or something.'

'You cook it, I'll be there.'

'You can buy a licence,' Julie went on. 'And we can be married as soon as we like. Dad's office will find out for you, tell you how to go about it.'

'I can find out unaided, thank you,' Toby said crisply.

'All right. Let's tell them, then.'

So they told them.

At first Veronica refused to take them seriously. 'Don't be silly,' she said. 'There's an immense amount to arrange. You can't possibly be married in a week or two. Ridiculous.'

'Just leave it to us. Don't worry,' Julie said airily.

'But – but what about – how am I to – oh, you don't understand at all what's involved. What on earth are you going to do about the cake, for instance?'

'Don't know. Haven't thought yet.' Julie remained confident. 'Harrods,' she added, inspiration visiting her.

'Where do you propose to be married,

then?' Max asked. 'London?'

Veronica was horrified. '*Not* in London,' she repeated, aghast. 'You aren't going to be married at Caxton Hall, are you?' Evidently this would be the final blow.

'Oh no, Mother. Here. At St Nicholas, I mean.'

'And where are you going to live?'

'With Toby, of course,' Julie said, surprised. 'In his flat. I shall simply be Mrs Toby Grant, the wife of one of the registrars. No one will realize for a moment I have any connection with the Hilliard miniatures at Alnaker Hall. Not that I would suppose anyone is going to be after them again in a hurry, after that fiasco.'

Max, who didn't share her confidence, had already evolved his own remedy. 'There aren't in future going to be any Alnaker pictures at all for them to be after,' he said sombrely.

Three faces turned as one.

Only Veronica found her voice. 'No Alnaker pictures?' she echoed.

'No. Oh, I know. They're beautiful, historic, valuable. But not worth the life of any of the family. I'm not having men on the security staff risked to save them, either. Or Mrs Hodgson, bless her. They'll have to go.'

'But what are you going to do with them?'

'Distribute them. Where there's hanging space, and they want them. The Tate, the National Gallery, the provincial art galleries. Some of the National Trust houses. We can pay our entrance fees, go and look at them occasionally, instead of worrying our guts out over them.'

His family looked at him in silence.

Craftily, he added, 'We can keep the Annigoni, I dare say. It may have considerably more impact, hung in solitary grandeur.' He raised his eyebrows, at his wife, winked at his daughter.

Veronica was taken by the notion of seeing herself alone in her glory. 'I suppose the gallery might look quite interesting with mirrors instead of pictures,' she admitted. 'Like Versailles, you know. Perhaps we should have the panelling stripped at the same time. Make it all light and airy, modern. New curtains, of course. And we could repaint the ceiling, too. Yes, I can see quite a few possibilities.'

She was safely diverted, Julie saw, the wedding relegated to a far corner of her mind.

And so, only three weeks later, Julie Alnaker and Toby Grant were married in the parish church of St Nicholas across the park, where they had both been christened.

The bride walked up the aisle on her father's arm, and down it on her husband's, as is customary. Not very fast, but steadily and without her sticks.

This Large Print Book, for people
who cannot read normal print,
is published under the auspices of

THE ULVERSCROFT FOUNDATION